Madison Julius Cawein

Days and dreams

Madison Julius Cawein

Days and dreams

ISBN/EAN: 9783743311718

Manufactured in Europe, USA, Canada, Australia, Japa

Cover: Foto ©Andreas Hilbeck / pixelio.de

Manufactured and distributed by brebook publishing software
(www.brebook.com)

Madison Julius Cawein

Days and dreams

CONTENTS.

ONE DAY AND ANOTHER.

I.

He waits musing.

HEREIN the dearness of her is :
 The thirty perfect days of June
 Made one, in beauty and in bliss
Were not more white to have to kiss,
 To love not more in tune.

And oft I think she is too true,
 Too innocent for our day ;
For in her eyes her soul looks new—
Two crowfoot-blossoms watchet-blue
 Are not more soft than they.

So good, so kind is she to me,
  In darling ways and happy words,
Sometimes my heart fears she may be
Too much with God and secretly
  Sweet sister to the birds.

2.

Becoming impatient.

The owls are quavering, two, now three,
  And all the green is graying ;
The owls our trysting dials be—
  There is no time for staying.

I wait you where this buckeye throws
  Its tumbled shadow over
Wood-violet and the bramble-rose,
  Long lady-fern and clover.

Spice-seeded sassafras weighs deep
  Rough rail and broken paling,
Where all day long the lizards sleep
  Like lichen on the railing.

Behind you you will feel the moon's
   Gold stealing like young laughter ;
And mists—gray ghosts of picaroons—
   Its phantom treasure after.

And here together, youth and youth,
   Love will be doubly able ;
Each be to each as true as truth,
   And dear as fairy fable.

The owls are calling and the maize
   With fallen dew is dripping—
Ah, girlhood, through the dewy haze
   Come like a moonbeam slipping.

3.

He hums.

There is a fading inward of the day,
   And all the pansy sunset hugs one star ;
To eastward dwindling all the land is gray,
   While barley meadows westward smoulder far.

Now to your glass will you pass
For the last time?
Pass,
Humming that ballad we know?—
Here while I wait it is late
And is past time—
Late,
And love's hours they go, they go.

There is a drawing downward of the night;
The wedded Heaven wends married to the
Moon;
Above, the heights hang golden in her light,
Below, the woods bathe dewy in the June.

There through the dew is it you
Coming lawny?
You,
Or a moth in the vines?
You!—at your throat I may note
Twinkling tawny,
Note,
A glow-worm, your brooch that shines.

4.

She speaks.

How many smiles in the asking ?—
　Herein I can not deceive you ;
My " yes " in a " no " was a-masking,
　Nor thought, dear, once to grieve you.
I hid.　The humming-bird happiness here
Danced up i' the blood　.　.　.　but what are
　　words
When the speech of two souls all truth affords ?
Affirmative, negative what in love's ear ?—
I wished to say " yes " and somehow said " no " ;
The woman within me knew you would know,
　　For it held you six times dear.

He speaks.

So many hopes in a wooing !—
　Therein you could not deceive me ;
The heart was here and the hope pursuing,
　Knew that you loved, believe me.—

Bunched bells o' the blush pomegranate—to fix
At your throat ; three drops of fire they are ;
And the maiden moon and the maiden star
Sink silvery over yon meadow ricks.
Will you look ?—till I hug your head back, so—
For I know it is "yes" though you whisper
    "no,"—
    And my kisses, sweet, are six.

5.

She speaks.

Could I recall every joy that befell me
There in the past with its anguish and bliss,
Here in my heart it has whispered to tell me,
    These were no joys to this.

Were it not well if our love could forget them,
Veiling the *was* with the dawn of the *is ?*
Dead with the past we should never regret them,
    These were no joys to this.

When they were gone and the present stood
    speechful,
Ardent with word and with look and with kiss,
What though we know that their eyes are beseech-
    ful,
      These were no joys to this.

Is it not well to have more of the spirit,
Living high futures this earthly must miss?
Less of the flesh with the past pining near it?—
      Such is the joy of this.

6.

She sings.

    We will leave reason,
    Dear, for a season ;
    Reason were treason
      Since yonder nether
    Foot-hills are clad now
    In nothing sad now ;
    We will be glad now,
      Glad as this weather.

Heart and heart ! in the Maytime, Maytime,
Youth and Love take playtime, playtime.   .
I in the dairy ; you are the airy
Majesty passing ; Love is the fairy
    Bringing us two together.

He sings.

    Starlight in masses
    Of mist that passes,
    Stars in the grasses ;
        Star-bud and flower
    Laughingly know us ;
    Secretly show us
    Earth is below us
        And for the hour
Soul has soul.   In the Maytime, Maytime,
Youth and Love take playtime, playtime.
You are a song ; a singer I hear it
Whispered in star and in flower ; the spirit,
    Love, is the power.

7.

He speaks.

And say we can not wed us now,
　Since roses and the June are here,
Meseems, beneath the beechen bough
　'T is just as sweet, my doubly dear,
To swear anew each old love vow,
　And love another year.

When breathe green woodlands through and
　　　through
　Wild scents of heliotrope and rain,
Where deep the moss mounds cool with dew,
　Beyond the barley-blowing lane,
More wise than wedding, is to woo—
　So we will woo again.

All night I lie awake and mark
　The hours by no clanging clock,
But in the dim and dewy dark
　Far crowing of some punctual cock ;
Until the lyric of the lark
　Mounts and Morn's gates unlock.

And would you be a nun and miss
    All this delightful ache of love?
Not have the moon for what she is?
    Love's honey-horn God holds above—
No world, for worlds are in a kiss
    If worlds are good enough.

So say we can not wed us now,
    Since roses and the June are here
We 'll stroll beneath the doddered bough,
    Heaven's mated songsters singing near,
To swear anew each old love vow,
    And love another year.

8.

He opens his heart.

And had we lived in the days
Of the Khalif Haroun er Reshid,
We had loved, as the story says,
Did the Sultan's favorite one
And the Persian Emperor's son
Ali ben Bekkar, he
Of the Kisra dynasty.

Do you know the story well
Of the Khalif Haroun's sultana?—
When night on the palace fell,
A slave through a secret door,
Low-arched on the Tigris' shore,
By a hidden winding stair
Ben Bekkar brought to his fair?

Then there was laughter and mirth,
And feasting and singing together,
In a chamber of marvellous worth;
In a chamber vaulted high
On columns of ivory;
Its dome, like the irised skies,
Mooned over with peacock eyes;
And the curtains and furniture,
Damask and juniper.

Ten slave-girls—so many blooms—
Stand sconcing tamarisk torches,
Silk-clad from the Irak looms;
Ten handmaidens serve the feast,
Each like to a star in the East;

Ten singers, their lutes a-tune,
Each like to a bosomed moon.

For her in the stuff of Merv
Blue-clad, unveiled, and jewelled,
No metaphor made may serve ;
Scarved deep with her own dark hair,
The jewels like fire-flies there—
Blossom and moon and star,
The Lady Shemsennehar.

The zone embracing her waist,—
The ransom of forty princes,—
But her form more priceless is placed ;
Carbuncles of Istakhar
In her coronet burning are—
Though gems of the Jamshid race,
Far rarer the gem of her face.

Tall-shaped like the letter I,
With a face like an Orient morning ;
Eyes of the bronze-black sky ;

Lips, of the pomegranate split,
With the light of her language lit ;
Cheeks, which the young blood dares
Make blood-red anemone lairs.

Kohled with voluptuous look,
From opaline casting-bottles,
Handmaidens over them shook
Rose-water, and strewed with bloom
Mosaics old of the room ;
Torch-rays on the walls made bars,
Or minted down golden dinars.

Roses of Rocknabad,
Hyacinths of Bokhara ;—
Not a spray of cypress sad ;—
Narcissus and jessamine o'er
Carved pillar and cedarn door ;
Pomegranates and bells of clear
Tulips of far Kashmeer.

And the chamber glows like a flower
Of the Tuba, or vale of El Liwa ;

And the bronzen censers glower ;
And scents of ambergris pour
With myrrh brought out of Lahore,
And musk of Khoten, and good
Aloes and sandal-wood.

Rubies, a tragacanth-red,
Angered in armlet and anklet
Dragon-like eyes that bled :
Bangles and necklaces dangled
Diamonds, whose prisms were angled,
Over veil and from coiffure, each
Or apricot-colored or peach.

And Ghoram now smites her lute,
Sings loves of Mejnoon and Leila,
Or amorous ghazals may suit :—
And the flambeaux snap and wave
Barbaric on free and slave,
Rich fabrics and bezels of gems,
And roses in anadems.

Sherbets in ewers of gold,
Fruits in salvers carnelian ;
Flagons of grotesque mold,
Made of a sapphire glass,
Stained with wine of Shirâz ;
Shaddock and melon and grape
On plate of an antique shape :

Vases of frost and of rose,
An alabaster graven,
Filled with the mountain snows ;
Goblets of mother-of-pearl,
One filigree silver-swirl ;
Vessels of gold foamed up
With spray of spar on the cup.—

When a slave bursts in with the cry :
" The eunuchs ! the Khalif's eunuchs !
With scimitars bared draw nigh !
Wesif and Afif and he,
Chief of the hideous three,
Mesrour ! the Sultan 's seen
'Mid a hundred weapons' sheen ! "   .   .   .

We, never had parted, no !
As parted those lovers fearful ;
But kissing you so and so,
When they came they had found us dead
On the flowers our blood dyed red ;
Our lips together and
The dagger in my hand.

9.
She speaks, musing.

O cities built by music ! lyres of love
   Strung to a songful sea ! did I but own
   One harp chord of one broken barbiton
What had I builded for our life thereof ?

In docile shadows under bluebell skies
   A home upon the poppied edge of eve,
   Beneath lone peaks the splendors never leave,
In lemon orchards whence the egret flies.

Where pitying gray the pitiless eyes of Death
   Blight no slight bud unfostered, I have thought
   Deep, lily-deep, pearl-pale daturas, fraught
With dewy fragrance like an angel's breath.

Sleep in the days ; the twilights tuned and tame
  Through mockbirds throating to attentive stars ;
  Each morn outrivalling each in opal bars ;
Eves preaching beauty with rose-tongues of flame.

O country by the undiscovered sea !
  The dream infolds thee and the way is dim—
  With head not high, what if I follow him,
Love—with the madness and the melody ?

10.

He, after a pause, lightly.

  An elf there is who stables the hot
  Red wasp that stings o' the apricot ;
  An elf who rowels his spiteful bay,
  Like a mote on a ray, away, away ;
  An elf who saddles the hornet lean
  To din i' the ear o' the swinging bean ;
  Who hunts with a hat cocked half awry
  The bottle-blue o' the dragon-fly :—
  O ho, O hi ! Oh, well know I.

An elf there is where the clover tips
A horn whence the summer leaks and drips,
Where lanthorns of mustard-flowers bloom,
In the dusk awaits the bee's dull boom ;
Gay gold brocade from head to knee,
Who robs the caravan bumble-bee ;
Big bags of honey bee-merchants pay
To the bandit elf of the Fairy way,—
O ho, O hey ! I have heard them say.

Another ouphen the butterflies know,
Who paints their wings like the buds that blow ;
Flowers, staining the dew-drops through,
Seals their colors in tubes of dew ;
Colors to dazzle the butterflies' wing—
The evening moth is another thing :
The butterfly's glory he got at dawn,
The moon-moth's got when the moon was wan ;
He it is, that the hollyhocks hear,
Who dangles a brilliant i' each one's ear ;
Teases at noon the pane's green fly,
And lights at night the glow-worm's eye :—
O ho, O hi ! Oh, well know I.

But the dearest elf, so the poets say,
Is the elf who hides in an eye of gray ;
Who curls in a dimple and slips along
The strings of a lute or a lover's song ;
Shines in a scent, or wings a rhyme,
And laughs in the bells of a wedding chime ;
Hides unhidden, where none may know,
In her bosom's blossom or throat's blue bow—
O ho, O ho !—a friend or foe ?

II.

She, seriously.

Who the loser, who the winner,
　　If the Fancy fail as preacher ?—
None who loved was yet beginner
　　Though another's love-beseecher ;
Love's revealment 's of the inner
　　Life and deity, the teacher.

Who may falsify the feeling
　　To the lover who is loser ?—

Has she felt :—the mere revealing
   Of the passion 's his accuser ;
She conceals it ; the concealing
   Is her own love's self-abuser.

One hath said, no flower knoweth
   Of the fragrance it revealeth ;
Song, its soul that overfloweth,
   Never nightingale's heart feeleth—
Such the love the spirit groweth,
   Love unconscious if it healeth.

12.

He.

Handsels of anemones
   The surrendered hours
Pour about the sweet Spring's knees—
Crowding babies of the breeze,
   Her unstudied flowers.

When 't is dawn, bestowing Day
   Strews with coins of golden

Every furlong of his way—
Like a Sultan gone to pray
　At a Kaaba olden.

Warlock Night, when dips the dark,
　Opens, tire on tire,
Windows of an heavenly ark,
Whence the stars swarm, spark on spark,
　Butterflies of fire.

With the night, the day, the spring,—
　Godly chords of beauty,—
We the instrument will string
Of our lives and love shall sing
　Songs of truth and duty.

13.

She.

How it was I can not tell,
　For I know not where nor why,
And the beautiful befell
　In a land that does not lie

East or West where mortals dwell—
   But beneath a vaguer sky.

Was it in the golden ages,
   Or the iron, that I heard,
In prophetic speech of sages,
   How had come a snowy bird
'Neath whose wing lay written pages
   Of an unknown lover's word ?

I forget ; you may remember
   How the earthquake shook our ships ;
How our city, one huge ember,
   Blazed within the thick eclipse ;
When you found me—deep December
   Sealed on icy eyes and lips.

I forget.   No one may say
   Pre-existences are true :
Here 's a flower dies to-day,
   Resurrected blooms anew :
Death is dumb and Life is gray—
   Who shall doubt what God can do !

14.

He.

As to this, nothing to tell,
 You being all my belief ;
Doubt may not enter or dwell
 Here where your image is chief,
Royal, to quicken or quell,
 Swaying no sceptre of grief.

Wise with the wisdom of Spring—
 Dew-drops, a world in each prism,
Gems from the universe ring :—
 Free of all creed and all schism,
Buds that are speechless but bring
 God-uttered God aphorism.

See how the synod is met
 There of the planets to preach us—
Freed from the frost's oubliette,
 Here how the flowers beseech us—
Were it not well to forget
 Winter and night as they teach us ?

Dew-drop, a bud, and a star,
   These—each a separate thought
Over man's logic how far !—
   God to a unit hath wrought—
Love, making these what they are,
   For without love they were naught.

Millions of stars ; and they roll
   Over your path that is white,
Here where we end the long stroll.—
   Seen of the innermost sight,
All of the love of my soul
   Kisses your spirit.   Good-night.

PART II.

I.

She delays, meditating.

Sad skies and a foggy rain
Dripping from streaming eaves ;
Over and over again
Dead drop of the trickling leaves ;
And the woodward winding lane,
And the hill with its shocks of sheaves,
    One scarce perceives.

Must I go in such sad weather
By the lane or over the hill ?
Where the splitting milk-weed's feather
Dim, diamond-like rain-drops fill ?
Or where, ten stars together,
Buff ox-eyes rank the rill
    By the old corn-mill ?

The creek by this is swollen,
And its foaming cascades sound ;
And the lilies, smeared with pollen,
In the race look dull and drowned ;—
'T is the path we oft have stolen
To the bridge, that rambles round
    With willows crowned.

Through a bottom wild with berry
Or packed with the iron-weeds,
With their blue combs washed and very
Purple ; the sorghum meads
Glint green near a wilding cherry ;
Where the high wild-lettuce seeds
    The fenced path leads.

A bird in the rain beseeches ;
And the balsams' budding balls
Smell drenched by the way which reaches
The wood where the water falls ;
Where the warty water-beeches
Hang leaves one blister of galls,
    The mill-wheel drawls.

My shawl instead of a bonnet ! . . .
Though the wood be soaking yet
Through the wet to the rock I 'll run it—
How sweet to meet in the wet !—
Our rock with the vine upon it,
Each flower a fiery jet—. . .
    He won't forget !

2.

He speaks, rowing.

Deep are the lilies here that lay
Lush, lambent leaves along our way,
Or pollen-dusty bob and float
White nenuphars about our boat
This side the woodland we have reached ;
Two rapid strokes our skiff is beached.

There is no path. Heaped foxgrapes choke
Huge trunks they wrap. This giant oak
Floods from the Alleghanies bore
To wedge here by this sycamore ;
Its wounded bulk, heart-rotted white,
Lights ghostly foxfire in the night.

Now oar we through this willow fringe
The bulging shore that bosks,—a tinge
Of green mists down the marge ;—where old,
Scarred cottonwoods build walls of shade
With breezy balsam pungent ; bowled
Around vined trunks the floods have made
Concentric hollows.   On we pass.

As we pass, we pass, we pass,
In daisy jungles deep as grass,
A bubbling sparrow flirts above
In wood-words with its woodland love :
A white-streaked woodpecker afar
Knocks : slant the sun dashed, each a star,
Three glittering jays flash over : slim
The piping sand-snipes skip and skim
Before us : and a finch or thrush—
 Who may discover where such sing ?—
The silence rinses with a gush
 Of mellow music gurgling.

On we pass, and onward oar
To yon long lip of ragged shore,

Where from yon rock spouts, babbling frore
A ferny spring ; where dodging by
Rests sulphur-disced that butterfly ;
Mallows, rank crowded in for room,
'Mid wild bean and wild mustard bloom ;
Where fishers 'neath those cottonwoods
    Last Spring encamped those ashes say
And charcoal boughs.—'T is long till buds !—
    Here who in August misses May ?

3.

He speaks, resting.

Here the shores are irised ; grasses
Clump the water gray that glasses
Broken wood and deepened distance :
Far the musical persistence
Of a field-lark lingers low
In the west where tulips blow.

White before us flames one pointed
Star ; and Day hath Night anointed

King ; from out her azure ewer
Pouring starry fire, truer
Than true gold.   Star-crowned he stands
With the starlight in his hands.

Will the moon bleach through the ragged
Tree-tops ere we reach yon jagged
Rock, that rises gradually ?
Pharos of our homeward valley.
Down the dusk burns golden-red ;
Embers are the stars o'erhead.

At my soul some Protean elf is :
You 're Simaetha, I am Delphis ;
You are Sappho and her Phaon—
I.   We love.   There lies a ray on
All the dark Æolian seas
'Round the violet Lesbian leas.

On we drift.   He loves you.   Nearer
Looms our island.   Rosier, clearer
The Leucadian cliff we follow,
Where the temple of Apollo

Lifts a pale and pillared fire—
Strike, oh, strike the Lydian lyre ;
Out of Hellas blows the breeze
Singing to the Sapphic seas.

4.

He sings.

Night, Night, 't is night.   The moon before to love
    us,
  And all the moonlight tangled in the stream :
Love, love, my love, and all the stars above us,
  The stars above and every star a dream.

In odorous purple, where the falling warble
  Of water cascades and the plunged foam glows,
A columned ruin heaps its sculptured marble
  Curled with the chiselled rebeck and the rose.

She sings.

Sleep, Sleep, sweet Sleep sleeps at the drifting
    tiller,
  And in our sail the Spirit of the Rain—

Love, love, my love, ah bid thy heart be stiller,
  And, hark ! the music of the harping main.

What flowers are those that blow their balm unto
    us ?
  Bow white their brows' aromas each a flame?
Ah, child, too kind the love we know, that knew
    us,
  That kissed our eyes that we might see the same.

He.

Night ! night ! good night ! no dream it is to vanish,
  The temple and the nightingale are there ;
The thornless roses bruising none to banish,
  The moon and one wild poppy in thy hair.

She.

Night ! night ! good night ! and love's own star be-
    fore thee,
  And love's star-image in the starry sea ;
Yes, yes, ah yes ! a presence to watch o'er thee—
  Night ! night ! good night and good the gods to
    thee !

5.

Homeward through flowers : she speaks.

O simple offerings of the common hills ;
Love's lowly names, that make you trebly sweet !
One Johnny-jump-up, but an apron-full
Of starry crowfoot, making mossy dells
Dim with heaven's morning blue ; dew-dripping
      plumes
Of waxen "dog-mouths " ; red the tippling cups
Of gypsy-lilies all along the creek,
Where dull the freckled silence sleeps, and dark
The water runs when, at high noon, the cows
Wade knee-deep and the heat hums drowsy with
The drone of dizzy flies ;—one Samson-flower
Blue-streaked and crystal as a summer's cloud ;
White violets, milk-weed, scarlet Indian-pinks,
All fragile-scented and familiar as
Pink baby faces and blue infant eyes.

O fair suggestions of a life more fair !
Love's fragrant whispers of an untaught faith,
High habitations 'neath a godlier blue

Beyond the sin of Earth, in heavens prepared—
What is it?—halcyon to utter calm,
Faith? such as wrinkled wisdom, doubting, has
Yearned for and sought in miser'd lore of worlds,
And vainly?—Love?—Oh, have I learned to live?

6.

He speaks.

Would you have known it seeing it?
Could you have seen it being it?
Waving me out of the budding land
Sunbeam-jewelled a bloom-white hand,
Wafting me life and hope and love,
Life with the hope of the love thereof,
    Love.

—" What is the value of knowing it? "—
Only the worth of owing it;
Need of the bud contents the light;
Dew at dawn and nard at night,
Beauty, aroma, honey at heart,
Which is debtor, part for part,
    Heart?

Thoughts, when the heart is heedable,
Then to the heart are readable ;
I in the texts of your eyes have read
Deep as the depth of the living dead,
Measures of truth in unsaid song
Learned from the soul to haunt me long,
            Song.

Love perpends each laudable
Thought of the soul made audible,
Said in gardens of bliss or pain :
Moonlight rays in drops of rain,
Feels the faith in its sleep awake,
Wish of the silent words that shake
            Sleep.

7.

She hums and muses.

If love I have had of thee thou hadst of me,
  No loss was in giving it over ;
Could I give aught but that I had of thee,
  Being no more than thy lover ?

And let it cease.   When what befalls befalls,
   You cannot love me less,
Loving me much now.   Neither weeks nor walls,
   With bitterest distress,

Shall all avail.   Despair will find reprieve,
   Though dark the soul be tossed,
In past possession of that love you grieve,
   The love which you have lost.

Ponder the morning, or the midnight moon,
   The wilding of the wold,
The morning slitting from night's brown cocoon
   Wide wings of flaxen gold :

The moon that, had not darkness been before,
   Had never shone to lead ;
And think that, though you are, you are not poor,
   Since you have loved indeed.

From flower to star read upward ; you shall see
   The purposes of loss,
Deep hierograms of gracious deity,
   And comfort in your cross.

8.

She speaks.

Sunday shall we ride together?
   Not the root-rough, rambling way
   Through the woods we went that day,
In the sultry summer weather,

Past the Methodist Camp-Meeting,
   Where religion helped the hymn
   Gather volume, and a slim
Minister with textful greeting

Welcomed us and still expounded.
   From the service on the hill
   We had rode three hills and still
Far away the singing sounded.

Nor that road through weed and berry
   Drowsy days led me and you
   To the old-time barbecue,
Where the country-side made merry.

Dusty vehicles together ;
  Darkies with the horses by
  'Neath the soft Kentucky sky,
And a smell of bark and leather ;

When you smiled, "Our modern tourney :
  Gallantry and politics
  Dinner, dance and intermix."
As we went the homeward journey

'Twixt hot chaparrals and thickets,   ·
  Heard brisk fiddles, scraping still,
  Drone and thump the quaint quadrille,
Like a worried band of crickets.—

Neither road.   The shady quiet
  Of that way by beech and birch,
  Winding to the ruined church
On the Fork that sparkles by it.

Where the silent Sundays listen
    For the preacher whom we bring,
    In our hearts to preach and sing
Week-day shade to Sabbath glisten.

9.

He, at parting.

Yes, to-morrow ; when the morn,
    Pentecost of flame, uncloses
Portals that the stars adorn,
    Whence a golden presence throws his
    Fiery swords and burning roses
At the wide wood's world of wall,
Spears of sparkle at each fall ;

Then together let us ride
    Down deep-wood cathedral places,
Where the pilgrim wild-flowers hide,
    Praying Sabbath in their faces ;
    Where in truest untaught phrases,
Worship in each rhythmic word,
Sings no migratory bird . . .

Pearl on pearl the high stars dight
   Jewels of divine devices
'Round the Afric throat of Night ;
   Where yon misty glimmer rises
   Soon the white moon crystallizes
Out of darkness, like a spell.—
Late, 't is late.   Till dawn, farewell.

PART III.

I.

Now rests the season in forgetfulness,
 Careless in beauty of maturity ;
 The ripened roses 'round brown temples, she
Fulfils completion in a dreamy guess :
Now Time grants night the more and day the less ;
 The gray decides ; and brown
Dim golds and reds in dulling greens express
 Themselves and broaden as the year goes
  down.
Sadder the croft where, thrusting gray and high
Their balls of seeds, the hoary onions die,
Where, Falstaff-like, buff-bellied pumpkins lie :
 Deeper each wilderness ;
Sadder the blue of hills that lounge along
The lonesome west ; sadder the song
Of the wild red-bird in the leafage yellow,
 Deeper and dreamier, aye !

Than woods or waters, leans the languid sky
Above lone orchards where the cider-press
    Drips and the russets mellow.

Nature grows liberal ; under woodland leaves
    The beech-nuts' burs their little pockets poke,
    Plump with the copper of the nuts that choke ;
Above our bristling way the spider weaves
A glittering web for which the Dawn designs
    Thrice twenty rows of sparkles. By the oak,
That rolls old roots in many gnarly lines,
    The acorn thimble, smoothly broke,
Shines by its saucer. On sonorous pines
The far wind organs ; but the forest here
    To no weak breeze hath woke ;
Far off the wind, but crumbling near and near,—
Each tingling twig expectant, and the gray
Surmise of heaven pilots it the way,
    Rippling the leafy spines,
Until the wildwood, one exultant sway,
Booms, and the sunlight, arrowing through it, shines
    Visible applause you hear.

How glows the garden ! though the white mists
    keep
    The vagabond in flowers reminded of
    Decay that comes to slay in open love,
When the full moon hangs cold and night is deep,
Unheeding such their cardinal colors leap
    Gay in the crescent of the blade of death ;
Spaced innocents in swaths he weeps to reap,
    Waiting his scythe a breath,
To gravely lay them dead with one last sweep.—
    Long, long admire
Their splendors manifold :—
The scarlet salvia showered with spurts of fire ;
Cascading lattices, dark vines that creep,
Nightshade and cypress ; there the marigold
Burning—a shred of orange sunset caught
And elfed in petals that eve's goblins brought
From elfland ; there, predominant red,
    The dahlia lifts its head
By the white balsams' red-bruised horns of honey,
    In humming spaces sunny.
The crickets singing dirges noon and night
For morn-born flowers, at dusk already dead,

For dusk-dead flowers weep ;
While tired Summer white,
Where yonder aster whispering odor rocks,—
The withered poppies knotted in her locks,—
Sighs, 'mong her sleepy hollyhocks asleep.

2.

The hips were reddening on the rose,
　The haws hung slips of fire ;
We went the woodland way that goes
　Up hills of branch and briar.
The hooked thorn held her gown and seemed
　Imploring her be staying
The sunlight of herself that beamed
　Beside it gently swaying.

Low bent the golden saxifrage ;
　Its yellow bells like bangles
The foxglove fluttered. Like a page—
　From out the rail-fence angles—
With crimson plume the sumach, hosed
　In Lincoln green, attended
My lady of the elder, posed
　In blue-black jewels splendid.

And as we mounted up the hill
  The rocky path that stumbled
Spread smooth ; and all the day was still
  And odorous with umbled
Tops of wild-carrots drying gray ;
  And there, soft-sunned before us,
An orchard dwindling away
  With dappled boughs bent o'er us.

An orchard where the pippin fell
  Worm-bitten, bruised, and dusty ;
And hornet-stung, each like a bell,
  The Bartlett ripened rusty ;
The smell of tawny peach and plum,
  That offered luscious yellow ;
Of wasp and bee the hidden hum,
  Made all the warm air mellow.

And on we went where many-hued
  Hung wild the morning-glory,
Their blue balloons in shadows, dewed
  With frost-white dew-drops hoary ;

In bush and burgrass far away
   Beneath us stretched the valley,
Cleft by one creek that laughed with day
   And babbled musically.

The brown, the bronze, the gray, the red
   Of weed and briar ran riot
Flush to dark woodland walls that led
   To nooks of whispering quiet.
Long, feathering bursts of golden-rod
   Ran golden woolly patches—
Bloom-sunsets of the withered sod
   The dying summer catches.

Then o'er the hills, loose-tumbling rolled—
   O'erleaping expectation—
The sunset, flaming marigold,
   A system's conflagration :
And homeward turning, she and I
   Went as one self in being—
God met us in the earth and sky
   And Love had purged our seeing.

3.

Say, my dear, O my dear,
These are the eves for speaking ;
There is no wight will work us spite
Beneath the sunset's streaking.

Yes, my dear, O my dear,
These are the eves for telling ;
To walk together in starry weather
Ere springs o' the moon are welling.

O my dear, yes, my dear,
These are the dusks for staying ;
When twilight dreams of night who seems
Among long-purples praying.

" No, my dear ! "—" Yes, my dear ! "
These are the nights to kiss it
Times twice-a-twenty : they grow a-plenty
On lips that will not miss it.

4.

To dream where silence sleeps
A sorrow's sleep that sighs ;

Where all heaven's azure peeps
    Blue from one wildflower's eyes
Where, in reflecting deeps,—
    Of cloudier woods and skies,—
    Another gray world lies.

Divining God from things
    Humble as weeds and bees ;
From songs the free bird sings
    Learn all are vain but these ;
In light-delighted springs,
    Wise, star-familiar trees,
    Seek love's philosophies.

5.

Here where the days are dimmest,
Each old, big-hearted tree
Gives bounteous sympathy ;
Here where dead nights sit grimmest
In druid company ;
Here where the days are dimmest.

Leaves of my lone communion,
Leaves ; and the listening sigh
Of silence wanders by ;
While on my soul the union
Is—of the wood and sky—
Leaves of my lone communion.

And eyes with tears are aching,
While life waits wistfully
For love that may not be :
In visions vain of waking
Lives all it can not see.—
And eyes with tears are aching,
And eyes with tears are aching.

6.

And here alone I sit and see it so.
A vale of willows swelling into knobs,
A bulwark eastward.   Sloping low
Westward the scooping waters flow
Under a rocky culvert's arch that throbs
With clanging wheels of transient trains that go
3

Screaming to north and south.
Here all the weary waters, stagnant stayed,
Sleep at the culvert's mouth ;
The current's hungry hiccup still afraid,
Haply, that I should never know
The secret 'neath the striate scum o' the stream
The devil and the dream,
I, dropping gravels so the echo sob
Mocking and thin as music of a shade
In shades that wring from rocks a hollow woe,
Complaining phantoms of faint whispers rob.

There, up the valley where the lank grass leaps
Blades each a crooked kris,
The currents strike or miss
Dream melodies : No wide-belled mallow sleeps
Monandrous flowers oval as a kiss ;
No mandrake curling convolutions up
Loops heavy blossoms, each a conical cup
That swoons moon-nectar and a serpent's hiss ;
No tiger-lily, where the crayfish play,
Mirrors a savage face, a copper hue
Streaked with a crimson dew ;

No dragon-fly in endless error keeps
Sewing the pale-gold gown of day
With tangled stitches of a burning blue,—
Whose brilliant body but a needle is,
An azurn and incarnate ray :—
But here, where haunted with the shade,
The dull stream stales and dies,
Are beauties none or few,
Such sinister and new ;
And one at widest noon-gaze shrinks afraid
Beneath the timid skies ;
So, if you ask me why I answer this :—

You know not ; only where the kildees wade
There in the foamy scum,
There where the wet rocks ail,—
Low rocks to which the water-reptiles come,
Basking pied bodies in the brindled shade,—
Dim as a bubble's prism on the grail
Below, an angled sparkle rayed,
While lights and shadows aid
From breeze-blown clouds that lounge at sunny
     loss,

Deep down, a sense of wavy features quail
The heart; with lips that writhe and fade
And clench; tough, rooty limbs that twist and
        cross,
And flabby hair of smoky moss.

A brimstone sunset.   And at night
The twinkling flies in will-o'-the-wisp dance wheel
Through copse and open, all a gnomish green.
I hear the water, and the wave is white
There where the boulder plants a keel,
And each taunt ripple 's sheen.—
Where instant insects dot
The dark with spurts of sulphur—bright,
Beneath the hazy height,
No bitter-almond trees make wan the night,
Building bloom ridges of a ghostly lustre,
But white-tops tossing cluster over cluster :
Huge-seen within that twilight spot—
As if a hill-born giant, half asleep,
Had dropped his night-cap while he drove his
        sheep

Foldward through fallow browns
And foxy grays,—a something crowns
The knoll—is it the odorous peak
Of one June-savory timothy stack ?

Now, one dead ash behind,
A weak moon shows a withered cheek
Of Quaker quiet, wasted o'er the vines'
Appentice ruins roofing pillared pines :
Beyond these, back and back,
An oak-wood stretches black—
And here the whining were-wolves of the wind
Snuff snarling : but their eyes are blind,
Although their fangs are fierce ;
And though they never pierce
Beyond the bad, bedevilled woodland streak,
I hear them, yes, I hear
A padding o' footsteps near,
A prowling pant in ear
And can not fly !—yes !—no !—
What horror holds me ?—That uncoiling slow,
Sure, mastering chimera there,
Hooping firm unseen feelers 'round my neck—

A binding, bruising coil   .   .   .
The waters burn and boil ;
The fire-flies the dappled darkness fleck
With impish dabs of blazing wizard's oil   .   .
Deep, deep into the black eye of the beck
I stare, magnetic fixed, and little reck
If all the writhing shadow slips,
Dripping around me, to the eyes and hips,
Where grinning murder leers with lupine lips.

                    7.

What can it mean for me? what have I done to
         her?
I in our freedom of love as a sun to her ;
She to our liberty goddess and slumberless
Moon of the stars shining silver and numberless :
Who on my life, that was thorny and showery,
Came—and made dewyness ; smiled—and made
         flowery ;
Mine ! the affinitized one of humanity :
Mine ! the elected of soul over vanity—
What have I done to her, what have I done !

What can it mean for me ? what have I said to her ?
I, who have idolized, worshipped, and pled to her ;
Sung for her, laughed for her, sorrowed and sighed
     for her,
Lived for her, hated and gladly had died for her !
See ; she has written me thus ! she has written me—
Sooner would dagger or serpent had smitten me !
Would they had shrivelled or ever they'd read of it !
Eyes, that are wide to the bitterest dread of it—
What have I said to her, what have I said !

What shall I make of it, I, who am trembling
Fearful of loss ?—Oh, enamored, dissembling
Flame !—of the candle that burning, but guttering,
Flatters the moth that comes circling and fluttering
Out of the summer night ; trusting, importunate,
Quitting cool flowers for this—O unfortunate !—
Such has she been to me making me such to her,
Slaying me, saying I never was much to her—
What shall I make of it, what can I make !   .

Love, in thy everglades, moaning and motionless
Look, I have fallen ; the evil is potionless :

I, with no thought but the heavens that lock us in,
Set naked feet 'mid the cottònmouth, moccasin
Under wild-roses, the Cherokee, eying me :—
In the sweet blue with the egrets that, flying me,
Loosened like blooms from magnolias, rose slenderly
White and pale pink ; where the mocking-bird ten-
     derly
Sang, making vistas of mosses melodious,
Wandered unheeding my steps in the odious
Slime that was venom ; I followed the fiery
Violet curve of thy star falling wiry—
So was I lost in night, thus am undone ! . . .

Have I not told to her—living alone for her—
Purposed unfoldments of love I had sown for her
Here in the soil of my soul ? .their variety
Endless ; and ever she answered with piety.—
See ! it has come to this . . . all the tale's suavity
At the ninth chapter grows stupid with gravity ;
Duller than death all our beautiful history—
Close it !—the *finis* is more than a mystery.—
Yes, I will tell her this ; yes, I will tell.

8.

I seem to hear her speak and see
   That blue-hung room.   Her perfume comes
From lavender folds vined dreamily—
     A-blossom with brocaded blooms,—
     A stuff of Orient looms.

Again I hear her speak and back,
   Where steals the showery sunlight, piles
A whatnot dainty bric-a-brac
     Beside a tall clock ; each glazed tile's
     Blue-patterned profile smiles.

I hear her say, " Ah, had we known,
   Could what has been have ever been ?—
And now ! " . . . How hurt the hard ache shone
     In eyes whose sadness seemed to lean
     On something far, unseen !

And as in sleep my own self seems
   Outside my suffering self :   I flush
In mists of undetermined dreams ;
     Behold her musing in that hush
     Of lilac light and plush.

Smiling but tortured.   Yes, I feel
   Despite that face, not seeming sad,
In those calm temples thoughts like steel
   Remorseless bore.   I had gone mad
   Had I once deemed her glad.

Unconsciously, with eyes that yearn
   To pierce beyond the present far,
Searching some future hope, I turn ;—
   There in her garden one fierce star,
   Beyond the window's bar,—

Vermilion as a storm-sunk sun,—
   A phyllocactus ?—all the life
Of torrid middays in but one
   Rich crimson bloom—flames red as strife ;
   And near it, rankly rife—

Deep coreopsis ?—heavy hues
   Of soft seal-bronze and satiny gold,
Sway girandoles whose jets of dews
   Burn points of starlight diamond-cold,
   Warm-colored, manifold.—

She dare not speak ; I can not.   Yet
   An intercourse 'twixt brain and brain
Goes feverish on.—Crushed, smelling wet,
   Through silken curtains drift again
   Verbena-scents of rain.

I in the doorway turn and stay ;
   Angry her cameo beauty mark
Set in that smile—Oh ! will she say
   No farewell ? no regret ? one spark
   Of hope to cheer the dark ?

That sepia-sketch—conceive it so—
   A roguish head with jaunty eyes
Laughing beneath a rose-chapeau,
   Silk-masked, unmasking—it denies
   The full-faced flower surprise ;

Hung o'er her davenport. . . .   We read
   The true beneath the false ; perceive
The smile that hides the ache.—Indeed !
   Whose soul unmasks ? . . . not mine !—I grieve
   Here, here, but laugh and leave. . . .

9.

Beyond the knotty apple-trees
    That fade about the old brick-barn,
Its tattered arms and tattered knees
A scare-crow tosses to the breeze
    Among the shocks of corn.

All things grow gray in earth and sky ;
    The cold wind sounding drearily
Makes all the rusty branches fly ;
The rustling leaves a-rotting lie ;
    The year is waning wearily.

At night I hear the far wild geese
    Honk in frost-bitten heavens, under
Arcturus.   Though I seem to cease
Outside myself and sleep in peace,
    I drowse awake and wonder.

' I know torn thistles by the creek
    Hang hairy with the frost ; the tented
Brown acres of the corn stretch bleak
And ghostly in the moonlight, weak
    In hollows bitter-scented.

Dream back the ways we strolled at morn
  Through woods of summer ever singing ;
Moon-trysts beneath the crooked thorn,
The tasselled meads of cane and corn
  Their restless shadows swinging. . . .

I stand and oar our boat among
  The dripping lilies of the river ;
I reach her hat the grape-vine long
Struck in the stream ; we sing a song,
  That song . . . I wake and shiver.

And then my feverish mind reverts
  To our sad words and sadder parting
In days long gone ; and, oh ! it hurts
Within here, for the soul asserts
  Mine the fool fault from starting.

And I must lie awake and think
  Of her with such regrets as gladly
No unrebuking conscience shrink ;
And hear the wild-fowls' clangor sink
  Through plaintive starlight sadly.

When all are overflown and deep
　The stoic night is left forsaken,
For company I well would weep,
Since all my spirit fears to sleep,
　Sleep of such visions shaken.

Grave visions of dead deeds that flaw
　Our waking hours, ever haunting;
Else were we, lacking love and law,
Rude scare-crow things of sticks and straw
　Undaunted and undaunting

10.

The sun a splintered splendor was
　In sober trees that broke and blurred,
　　That afternoon we went together
In droning hum and whirling buzz,
　Where hard the dinning locust whirred,
　　Through fields of golden-rod a-feather.

So sweet it was to look and lean
　To your young face and feel the light
　　Of eyes that fondled mine unsaddened !

The laugh that left lips more serene ;
　The words that blossomed like the white
　　Life-everlasting there and gladdened.

Maturing Summer, you were fraught
　With wiser beauties then than now
　　Parades rich Autumn's red November ;
This stuns : there dreams no subtle thought
　As then on hinting bush and bough—
　　But now I am alone, remember.

II.

Through iron-weeds and roses
　And bronzing beech and oak,
Old porches it discloses,
Above the briars and roses
　Fall's feeble sunbeams soak.

Neglected walks that tangle
　The dodder-strangled grass ;
Its chimney shows one angle
Heaped with dead leaves that spangle
　The paths that round it pass.

The early mists that bury
  And hide them in its rooms,
From spider closets—very
Dim with old webs—will hurry
  Out in the raining glooms.

They haunt each stair and basement ;
  They stand on hearth and porch ;
Lean from each paneless casement,
Or in the moonlight's lacement
  Fly with a phantom torch.

There is a sense of frost here ;
  And gusts that sob away
Of something that was lost here,
Long, long ago was lost here,
  But what, they can not say.

There croons no owl to startle
  Despondency within ;
No raven o 'er its portal
To scare the daring mortal
  And guard its cellared sin.

The creaking road descries it
This side the dusty toll ;
The farmer passing eyes it ;
None stops t' philosophize it,
This symbol of a soul.

12.

Though the dog-tooth violet come
With the shower,
And the wild-bee haunt and hum
Every flower,
We shall never wend as when
Love laughed leading us from men
Over violet vale and glen,
Where the red-bird sang an hour,
And we heard the partridge drum.

Here October shadows pray,
Till one stills
Joyance, where for buried May
Sob the rills :

So love's vision has arisen
Of the long ago : I listen—
Memory, tears in eyes that glisten
Points but Indiana hills
Fading dark-blue far away

PART IV.

I.

When in her cloudy chiton
Spring freed the donjoned rills,
And trumpeting, a Triton,
Wind-war was on the hills ;
O'er ways, hope's buds bedizen,
Long ways the glory lies on,
Love spread us an horizon
Of gold beyond life's ills.

When Summer came with sickle
Stuck in a sheaf of gleams,
And eves were honey-trickle
From bee-hives of the beams ;
Scrolls of the days blue-blotted,
Scrolls of the night star-dotted,
To love and us allotted
A world of woven dreams.

When Autumn waited tired—
A fair-faced heretic—
Auto-de-fés Frost fired
In Winter's Bishopric ;
Our loves, a song had started,
Grew with the song sad-hearted,
Sweet loves long-sworn were parted,
Though life for love was sick.

Now is the Winter waited
'Neath skies of frozen gold,
Or raining heavens hated
Of winds that curse and scold.—
Shall this be so : that never
Shall sunlight snowlight sever?
Forever and forever
The heart wait winter-cold?

2.

Soft music bring that seems to weep
  All this dull sorrow of the soul ;
Vague music soft to utter sleep,
  Sleep and undying dole :

Forgetting not—forgotten most—
How love is well though lost.

So weary, oh ! and yet so fain
　　In silent service of the heart ;
Still feeling if it be in vain
　　Love's spirit hath His part ;
And if in death God grant the rest
Life were but kind at best.

3.

Last night I slept till midnight
　　Then woke, and far away
A cock crowed ; lonely and distant
　　Came mournful a watch-dog's bay ;
But lonelier, slower the tedious
　　Old clock ticked on towards day.

And what a day !—remember
　　The morns of a Summer and Spring,
That bound two lives together ?
　　Each morn a wedding ring
Of dew and dreams and sparkle,
　　Of flowers and birds a-wing ?

Broad morns when I strolled the garden
　　Awaiting one the rose
Expected, fresh in its blushes—
　　The Giant of Battle that grows
A head of radiance and fragrance,
　　The champion of the close.

Not in vain did I wait, departed
　　Summer, this morning mocks ;
'Mid the powdery crystal and crimson
　　Of your hollow hollyhocks ;
Your fairy-bells and poppies,
　　And the bee that in them rocks.

Cool-clad 'mid the pendulous purple
　　Of the morning-glory vine,
By the giant pearls pellucid
　　Of the peonies a-line,
The snapdragons' and the pansies'
　　Deep-colored jewel mine.

Shall I ever see my mealy,
　　Drunk dusty-millers gay ;
My lady-slippers bashful

Of butterfly and ray ;
My gillyflowers as spicy
    Each as a day of May ?

Oh, dear when I think of the handfuls
    Of little gold coin a-mass,
My bachelor's-buttons scatter
    Over the garden grass ;
Of the marigold that boasts its
    One bit of burning brass ;

More bitter I feel the winter
    Tighten to spirit and heart ;
And dream of the days remembered
    As lost—of the past a part ;
Of the ways we went, all blotted,
    'Tear-blotted on love's chart.

And I see the mill and the diamonds
    Of foam tossed from its wheel ;
Red lilies tumbled together,
    The madcap wind at heel ;
And the timid veronicas' blossoms—
    Those prayers the woods conceal.

The wild-cat gray of the meadows
   That the ox-eyed daisies dot,
Fawn-eyed and a leopard-yellow,
   That tangle a tawny spot—
As if some panther tired
   Lay dozing tame and hot.

Ah ! back again with the present,
   With winds that pinch and twist
Each leaf in their peevish passion,
   And whirl wherever they list ;
With the morning hoary and nipping,
   Whose mausolean mist

Builds white a tomb for the daylight—
   A frosty, shaggy fog,
That fits gray wigs on the cedars,
   And furs with wool each log ;
Carpets with satin the meadow,
   And velvets white the bog.

Alone at morn—indifferent ;
   Alone at eve—I sigh ;

And wait, like the wind complaining,
  Complain and know not why ;
But ailing and longing and hating
  Because I cannot die.

How dull are the sunsets ! dreary
  Cold, hard and harsh and dead !
Far richer were those of August,
  One stain of wine-dark red—
The juice of a mulberry vintage—
  To the new moon overhead.

But now I sit with the sighing
  Dead wests of a dying year !
Like the fallen leaves and the acorns
  Am worthless and feel as sear ;
For the soul and the body sicken,
  And the heart 's one scalding tear.

And I stare from my window ! The darkness,
  Like a bravo, his cloak throws on ;
The moon, like a hidden lanthorn,
  Glitters—or dagger drawn ;

4

All my heart cries out beseeching :
"Strike here ! strike and be gone ! "

4.

When friends are sighing
    Round one and one
Nearer is lying,
    Nearer the sun,
When one is dying
    And all is done ;

I may remember,
    You may forget
Words, each an ember,
    Burning here yet—
In dead December
    One will regret.

Love we have given,
    Over and o'er,
All, who has driven
    Us from his door,
Is he forgiven
    When he is poor ?

What if you wept once,
  What though he knew !
What if he slept once !
  Still he was true,
If he but kept once
  Something of you.

Never forgetful,
  Love may forget ;
Froward and fretful,
  Child, he will fret ;
Ever regretful,
  He will regret.

Love would be sweeter
  If we but knew ;
Lives be completer
  To themselves true ;
Hearts more in metre,
  Truth looking through.

Flesh never near it,
  Being impure,
Mind must endear it

Making it sure—
Love in the spirit,
  That will endure.

So when to-morrow
  Ceases and we
Quit this we borrow,
  Mortality,
Such chastens sorrow
  So it may see.

There will be weeping,
  Weary and deep,—
God's be the keeping
  Of those that weep !—
When our loved, sleeping,
  Sleep their long sleep ;

Then they are dearer
  Than we 're aware ;
Character clearer,
  Being more fair ;
Then they are nearer,
  Nearer by prayer.

5.

They will not say I can not live beyond the weary
  night,
But then I know that I shall die before comes
  morning's light.
How frail is flesh !—but you 'll forgive me now I
  tell you how
I loved you, love you ; and the pain it gives to
  leave you now ?

This could not be on earth ; the flesh, that clothes
  the soul of me—
Ordained at birth a sacrifice to this heredity—
Denied, forbade.—Ah, you have seen the bright
  spots in my cheeks
Grow hectic, as before comes night blood dyes the
  sunset's streaks ?

Consumption. " But I promised you my love "—
  't is left forlorn
Of life God summons unto him, and is it then for-
  sworn ?—

Oh, I was glad in love of you ; but think : if I had
    died
Ere babe of mine had come to be a solace at your
    side ?

Had it been little then, your grief, when Heaven
    had made us one
In everything that 's good on earth and then the
    good undone ?
No ! no !—and had I lived to raise a boy we saw
    each day
Bud into beauty, with that blight born in him that
    must slay !

Just when we cherish him the most, and youthful,
    sunny pride
Sits on his curly front, he pines and dies ere I have
    died.
Whose fault ?—not mine ! but hers or his, that an-
    cestor who gave
Escutcheon to our humble house—a death's-head
    and a grave.

Beneath the pomp of those grim arms we live and
    may not move ;
Nor faith, nor fame, nor wealth avail to hurl them
    down, nor love.
How could I tell you this ?—not then ! when all the
    world was spun
Of morning colors for our love to walk and dance
    upon.   -

I could not tell you how disease hid here a viper
    germ,
Precedence slowly claiming and so slowly fixing
    firm.
And when I broke our plighted troth and would
    not tell you why,
I loved you, thinking " time enough when I have
    come to die."

Draw off my rings and let my hands rest so .· . .
    the wretched cough
Will interrupt my feeble speech and will not be
    put off. . . .

Ah, anyhow, my anodyne is this—to feel that you
Are near me, that your healthy hand soothes mine's
    unhealthy dew.

And that your heart excuses all, and that you will
    not fret
Because you understand me now and never will
    forget.—
Now bring me roses pale and pure and tell me
    death 's a lie,
—Late was it hard for me to live, now it is hard to
    die.

PART V.

I.

Vased in her bedroom window, white
  As her glad girlhood, never lost,
I smelt the roses ; and the night
  Outside was fog and frost.

What though I claimed her dying there !
  God nor one angel understood
Nor cared, who from loved feet to hair
  Had changed to mist her blood.

Love, love had claimed us long, and long
  Our hearts sang harp-strung, late and soon ;
But God !—God jangles thus the song
  And makes discord of tune.

What lily lilier than her face !
  More virgin than her lips I kissed !
When morn like God, with gold and grace
  Broke massed in mist ! broke massed in mist !

2.

Love, to your face farewell now,
　Pillowed a flower on flowers ;
Eyes, white-weighed with a spell now ;
Lips, with nothing to tell now,
　That bade adieu to ours.

Dear, is your soul so daggered
　There by a world that hates ?
Love—is *he* ever laggard ?
Hope—is *her* face so haggard ?
　You, who are one with the Fates ?

Never to wait to-morrow
　Under such worldly skies !
Never to sleep with sorrow !
Hour by hour to borrow
　Joy that has only sighs !

Sweet, farewell forever ;
　And a burning tear or two—
Will they reach your knowledge ever,
And touch through the dreams that sever
　My life from the life of you ?

O Life, in my flesh so fearful
  Medicine me this pain !
Thy eyes with a science cheerful,
But mine, with a mystery tearful,
  Tearful and slumber-fain.

Love, to your lips farewell now—
  Your spirit through them I kiss ;
Lips—so sealed with a spell now !
Lips, with nothing to tell now
  But this ! but this ! but this ! . . .

3.

So long it seems since last I saw her face,
    So long ago it seems,
Like some sad soul, in unconjectured space,
Lost in the happiness of some dead grace
Remembered—I. And, oh ! a little while
The sorrow stabs and Death conceals no smile
From Love bowed weeping in a thorny place—
So long ago, our love is what are dreams !

Since she is gone no more I feel the light,
  Since she is gone beyond,
Burst like a revelation out of night,—
Golden convictions of far futures bright,—
Whiles clouds around the west take marble tones ;
For Hope sits sighing in a place of stones,
Dark locks dishevelled and face very white,—
Since she is gone and life 's an iron bond.

Now she is dead the doubt Love dulled with awe,
  Now she is dead to me,
Questions the wisdom of diviner law.
Self-solved of self I search to find a flaw—
O egotism of Earth's fools and slaves !—
For Faith leans thoughtful in a place of graves,
On that unseen from this seen known to draw,
Now she is dead and it is hard to see.

4.

Ridged and bleak the gray forsaken
  Twilight at the night has guessed,
Where no star of dusk has taken
  Flame unshaken in the west.

All the day the woodlands dying
  Moaned, and drippings as of grief
Tossed from barren boughs with sighing
  Death of flying twig and leaf.

Ah, to be a dream unbroken,
  Past the ironies of Fate !
Born a tree ; with branches oaken
  Dear unspoken intimate.

Who may say that man has never
  Lived the mighty hearts of trees ?
Graduating Godward ever,
  The Forever finds through these ?

Colors, we have lived, are cherished ;
  Odors, we have been, are ours ;
Entity alone has perished ;
  Beauty-nourished souls were flowers.

Music, when the fancy guesses,
  Lifts us loftier thoughts among ;
Spirit that the flesh distresses,
  But expresses self with song. . . .

Heaven in darkness bends upbraiding
  Without moonlight, without star ;
Darkness and the reason aiding,
  All but fading phantoms are.

Still philosophy is saying :
  " Now that hope with life seems gone,
Some are cursing, some are praying,
  God smiles raying in the dawn ! "

5.

Wild weather ; the whip of the sleet
  On the shuttered casement tapping ;
A shadow from face to feet,
  Like a shroud, my spirit wrapping,

Wild weather ; and how is she
  Now the sting of the storm beats serried,
Over the stone and the tree
  Of the grave where she is buried ?

Wild weather ; I cannot weep—
  But the skies weep on and worry ;
So I sleep, and dream in my sleep
  How I hear dim garments hurry. . . .

Star weather and footsteps of stars ;
　　And I see white raiment glisten,
Like the glow on the face of Mars
　　When the stars to the angels listen.

And with me I see how she stands
　　With lips high thought has weighted ;
With testifying hands,
　　And eyes with purity mated.

Have I spoken and have I kneeled
　　To the prayer I worship, I wonder ?—
What waits on her lips that are sealed ?
　　God-sealed and who shall sunder !

I sob, " Oh your stay was long !
　　You are come, but your feet were laggard,
With mansuetude and song
　　For a heart your death has daggered."

And I lift wet eyes to her
　　Unutterable with weeping,
And beg for the loves that were,
　　Now passed into Heaven's keeping. . . .

I wake and a clock tolls three—
   And the night and the storm lie serried
On the testament that 's she,
   Closed, clasped, and forever buried.

6.

The night is shrewd with storm and sleet ;
   Each loose-warped casement raps or groans ;
I hear the wailing woodland beat
   The tempest with long blatant moans,
Like one who fears defeat.

And sitting here beyond the storm,
   Alone within the lonely house,
It seems of Sleep the Fairy charm
   Weaves incantations ; even the mouse
That scratched has come to harm.

And in this grave light, stolen o'er
   Familiar objects, grown severe,
I 'm strange—as, opening a door,
   One finds one's dead self standing near,
One knew not dead before.

The old stair rings with growling gusts ;
   Each hearth's flue gasps a gorgon throat
That snores and sleeps ; the spectral dusts,
   Which yonder Shawnee war-gear coat,
Whose quiver hangs and rusts,

Are shaken ; till I feel that he,
   Who wore it in the wild war-dance,
And died in it, fills shadowy
   Its wampumed skins ; its plume, perchance,
Shakes, scowling eyes at me.

And so the Swedenborge I toss
   Aside, contented with the dark
That takes me.   O'er the fire-light cross ;
   Pass where the andirons spit and spark,
And ponder o'er her loss.

Or from the flaw-splashed window yearn
   Out toward the waste, where sway and dip
Dank, dark December boughs, where burn
   Some late last leaves, that icy drip
No matter where you turn.

Where sodden soil, you scarce have trod,
  Fills oozy footprints ; and the night
So ugly that it mocks at God,
  Creating monsters which the sight
Fancies, unseen, abroad.

The months I count : how long it seems
  Since that bland summer when with her,
There on her porch, in rainy gleams
  We watched the mellow lightning stir
In rain-clouds gray as dreams !

When all the west a torn gold sheet—
  Swift openings of some Titan's forge—
Laid bald with storm ; in quivering heat
  Pitched precipice and nightmare gorge,
Where thunder torrents beat.

And strong the wind was as again
  Storm lit the instant earth ; and how
The wood sprang out one virent stain ;
  We read no more—lost is it now !—
In *Romance of a Reign ;*

A tale of nowhere ; then that we
  Were reading till we heard the plunge
Of distant thunder sullenly,
  And left to mark long lightnings lunge
Convulsions fiery.

What worlds love wrought us, dreaming there,
  Of sorcery and necromance !
With spirits lustrous of the air,
  A land like one great pearl, a trance
Of floods and forests fair.

Where white-faced flowers sang and thought ;
  Where fragrant birds flew, brilliant-blown,
In winging odors ; feather-fraught
  With light, where breathing colors shone,
On throbbing music brought.

Or built us some snug country home
  Among the hills ; with terraces
Vine-hung and orchared o'er the foam
  Of the Ohio, far one sees
Wind crimson in the gloam.

And this ! and this !—alone ! alone !
    To hear the sweep of winter rain,
The missiled sleet's sharp arrows blown ;
    Dark shadow on the freezing pane,
And on my heart a moan !

DAYS AND DREAMS.

HE dreamed of hills so deep with woods
 Storm-barriers on the summer sky
Are not more dark, where plunged loud floods ·
 Down rocks of sullen dye.

Flat ways were his where sparsely grew
 Gnarled, iron-colored oaks, with rifts,
Between dead boughs, of Eden-blue :
 Ways where the speedwell lifts

Its shy appeal, and spreading far—
 The gold, the fallen gold of dawn
Staining each blossom's balanced star—
 Hollows of cowslips wan.

Where 'round the feet the lady-smock
 And pearl-pale lady-slipper creep ;
White butterflies upon them rock
 Or seal-brown suck and sleep.

At eve the west shoots crooked fire
　　Athwart a half-moon leaning low ;
While one white, arrowy star throbs higher
　　In curdled honey-glow.

Was it some elfin euphrasy
　　That purged his spirit so that there
Blue harebells, by those ways that be,
　　Seemed summoning to prayer ?

For all the death within him prays ;
　　Not he—his higher self, whose love
Fire-filled the flesh.　Its light still stays
　　Touched by the soul above.

They found him dead his songs beside,
　　Six stairs above the din and dust
Of life : and that for which he died
　　Denied him even a crust.

DEITY.

NO personal ; a God divinely crowned
  With gold and raised upon a golden throne
Deep in a golden glory, whence he nods
Man this or that—and little more than man !

And shalt thou see Him individual ?
Not till the freed intelligence hath sought
Ten hundred hundred years to rise and love,
Piercing the singing cycles under God,—
Their iridescent evolutions orbed
In wild prismatic splendors,—shall it see—
Through God-propinquity become a god—
See, lightening out of spheric harmonies,
Resplendencies of empyrean light,
Prisms and facets of ten million beams
Starring a crystal of berainbowed rays,
And in this—eyes of burning sapphire, eyes

Deep as the music of the beautiful ;
And o'er the eyes, limpid hierarchal brows,
As they were lilies of seraphic fire ;
Lips underneath, of trembling ruby—lips
Whose tongue 's a chord, and every sound a song :
Cherubic faces of intensity
In multiplying myriads to a word
Forming the unit—God ; Supremity
Creative and ubiquitous.

                    From this
Thy intellect, detached, expelled and breathed
Exaltant into flesh endowed with soul,
One sparkle of the Essence clothed with clay.—
O high development ! devolvings up
From matter to unmattered potencies,
Up to the source and fountain of all mind,
Beauty and truth, inviolable Love,
And so resumed and reabsorbed in God,
One more expression of eternity !

SELF.

A SUFI debauchee of dreams
　　Spake this :—From Sodomite to Peri
　　Earth tablets us ; we live and are
Man's own long commentary.

Is one begat in Bassora,
　　One lies in Damietta dying—
The plausibilities of God
　　All possibles o'erlying.

But burns the lust within the flesh ?—
　　Hell 's but a homily to Heaven,—
Put then the individual first,
　　And of thyself be shriven.

Neither in adamant nor brass
　　The scrutinizing eye records it ;
The arm is rooted in the heart,
　　The heart that rules and lords it.

7

Be that it is and thou art all ;
   And what thou art so thou hast written
Thee of the lutanists of Love,
   Or of the torture-smitten.

SELF AND SOUL.

IT came to me in my sleep,
   And I rose from my sleep and went
Out in the night to weep,
   Over the bristling bent.
With my soul, it seemed, I stood
Alone in a moaning wood.

And my soul said, gazing at me,
   "Shall I show you another land
Than other this flesh can see?"
   And took into hers my hand.—
We passed from the wood to a heath
As starved as the ribs of Death.

Three skeleton trees we pass,
   Bare bones on an iron moor,
Where every leaf and the grass
   Was a thorn and a thistle hoar.

And my soul said, looking on me,
" *The past of your life you see.*"

And a swine-herd passed with his swine,
   Deformed ; and I heard him growl ;
Two eyes of a sottish shine
   Leered under two brows as foul.
And my soul said, " *This is the lust
That soils my limbs with the dust.*"

And a goose wife hobbled by
   On a crutch, with the devil's geese ;
A-mumbling how life is a lie,
   And cursing my soul without cease.
And my soul said, " *This is desire ;
The meaning of life is higher.*"

And we came to a garden, close
   To a hollow of graves and tombs ;
A garden as red as a rose
   Hung over of obscene glooms ;
The heart of each rose was a spark
That smouldered or splintered the dark.

And I was aware of a girl
  With a wild-rose face, who came
With a mouth like a shell's split pearl,
  Rose-clad in a robe of flame ;
And she plucked the roses and gave,
And my flesh was her veriest slave.

She vanished. My lips would have kissed
  The flowers she gave me with sighs,
But they writhed in my hands and hissed,
  In their hearts were a serpent's eyes.
And my soul said, " *Pleasure is she ;*
The joys of the flesh you see."

And I bowed with a heart too weary,
  That longed for rest, for sleep ;
And my eyes were heavy and teary,
  And yearned for a way to weep.
And my soul smiled, " *This may be !*
Will you know me and follow me ?"

THE DREAM OF DREAD.

I HAVE lain for an hour or twain
   Awake, and the tempest is beating
On the roof, and the sleet on the pane,
   And the winds are three enemies meeting ;
And I listen and hear it again,
   My name, in the silence, repeating.

Then dumbness of death that must slay,
   Till the midnight is burst like a bubble ;
And out of the darkness a ray—
   'T is she ! the all beautiful double ;
With a face like the breaking of day,
   Eyes dark with the magic of trouble.

I move not ; she lies with her lips
   At mine ; and I feel she is drawing
My life from my heart to their tips,
   My heart where the horror is gnawing ;

My life in a thousand slow sips,
  My flesh with her sorcery awing.

She binds me with merciless eyes ;
  She drinks of my blood, and I hear it
Drain up with a shudder and rise
  To the lips, like the serpent's, that steer it
And she lies and she laughs as she lies,
  Saying, " Lo, thy affinitized spirit ! "

Then I hear—as if torturing swords
  Had shivered and torments had grated
Hoarse iron deep under ; and words
  As of sins that howled out and awaited
A fiend who lashed into their hords,
  And a demon who lacerated.

And I shriek and lie clammy and stark,
  As the curse of a devil mounts higher,
Up—out of damnation and dark,
  Up—a hobble of hoofs that is dire ;
I feel that his mouth is a spark,
  His features, of filth and of fire.—

" To thy body's corruption, thy grave !
   Thy hell ! from which thou hast stolen ! "
And a blackness rolls down like a wave
   With a clamor of tongues that are swollen—
And I feel that my flesh is the slave
   Of a—vampire, diakka, eidolon ?

DEATH IN LIFE.

WITHIN my veins it beats
     And burns within my brain ;
For when the year is sad and sear
     I dream the dream again.

Ah ! over young am I
God knows ! yet in this sleep
More pain and woe than women know
     I know, and doubly deep ! . . .

Seven towers of shaggy rock
     Rise red to ragged skies,
Built in a marsh that, black and harsh,
     To dead horizons lies.

Eternal sunset pours,
     Around its warlock towers,
A glowing urn where garnets burn
     With fire-dripping flowers.

O'er bat-like turrets high,
  Stretched in a scarlet line,
The crimson cranes through rosy rains
  Drop like a ruby wine.

Once in the banquet-hall
  These scarlet storks are heard :—
I sit at board with men o' th' sword
  And knights of noble word ;

Cased all in silver mail ;
  But he, I love and fear,
In glittering gold beside me bold
  Sits like a lover near.

Wild music echoes in
  The hollow towers there ;
Behind bright bars o' his visor, stars
  Beam in his eyes and glare.

Wild music oozes from
  Arched ceilings, caked with white
Groined pearl ; and floors like mythic shores
  That sing to seas of light.

Wild music and a feast,
And one's belovèd near
In burning mail—why am I pale,
So pale with grief and fear ?

Red heavens and slaughter-red
The marsh to west and east ;
Seven slits of sky, seven casements high,
Flare on the blood-red feast.

Our torches tall are these,
Our revel torches seven,
That spill from gold soft splendors old—
The hour of night—eleven.

No word.   The sparkle aches
In cups of diamond-spar,
That prism the light of ruddy white
In royal wines of war.

No word.   Rich plate that rays,
Splashes of splitting fires,
Off beryl brims ; while sobs and swims
Enchantment of lost lyres.

I lean to him I love,
And in the silence say :
"Would thy dear grace reveal thy face,
If love should crave and pray ? "

Grave Silence, like a king,
. At that strange feast is set ;
Grave Silence still as the soul's will,
That rules the reason yet.

But when I speak, behold !
The charm is snapped, for low
Speaks out the mask o' his golden casque,
"At midnight be it so ! "

And Silence waits severe,
Till one sonorous tower,
Owl-swarmed, that looms in glaring glooms,
Sounds slow the midnight hour.

Three strokes ; the knights arise,
The palsy from them flung,
To meward mock like some hoarse rock
When wrecking waves give tongue.

Six strokes ; and wailing out
The music hoots away ;
The fiery glimmer of eve dies dimmer,
The red grows ghostly gray.

Nine strokes ; and dropping mould
The crumbling hall is lead ;
The plate is rust, the feast is dust,
The banqueters are dead.

Twelve strokes pound out and roll ;
The huge walls writhe and shake
O'er hissing things with taloned wings—
Christ Jesus, let me wake !

Then rattling in the night
His iron visor slips—
In rotting mail a death's-head pale
Kisses my loathing lips.

Two hell-fierce lusts its eyes,
Sharp-pointed like a knife,
That flaming seem to say, " *No dream !*
No dream ! the truth of Life ! "

THE EVE OF ALL-SAINTS.

I.

THIS is the tale they tell,
    Of an Hallowe'en ;
This is the thing that befell
Me and the village Belle,
    Beautiful Aimee Dean.

2.

Did I love her ?—God and she,
    They know and I !
And love was the life of me—
Whatever else may be,
    Would God that I could die !

3.

That All-Saints' eve was dim ;
    The frost lay white
Under strange stars and a slim
Moon in the graveyard grim,
    An Autumn ghost of light.

4.

They told her : " Go alone,
    With never a word,
To the burial plot's unknown
Grave with the grayest stone,
    When the clock on twelve is heard ;

5.

" Three times around it pass,
    With never a sound ;
Each time a wisp of grass
And myrtle pluck, and pass
    Out of the ghostly ground ·

6.

" And the bridegroom that 's to be
    At smiling wait,
With a face like mist to see,
With graceful gallantry
    Will bow you to the gate."

7.

She laughed at this, and so
    Bespoke us how
To the burial place she 'd go :—
And I was glad to know,
    For I 'd be there to bow.

8.

An acre from the farm
    The homestead graves
Lay walled from sun and storm ;
Old cedars of priestly form
    Around like sentinel slaves.

9.

I loved, but never could say
  Such words to her,
And waited from day to day,
Nursing the hope that lay
  Under the doubts that were.—

10.

She passed 'neath the iron arch
  Of the legended ground,
And the moon like a twisted torch
Burned over one lonesome larch ;
  She passed with never a sound.

11.

Three times had the circle traced,
  Three times had bent
To the grave that the myrtle graced ;
Three times, then softly faced
  Homeward, and slowly went.

12.

Had the moonlight changed me so ?
  Or fear undone
Her stepping strange and slow ?
Did she see and did not know ?
  Or loved she another one ?

13.

Who knows ?—She turned to flee
  With a face so white
That it haunts and will haunt me ;
The wind blew gustily,
  The graveyard gate clanged tight

14.

Did she think it me or—what,
  Clutching her dress ?
Her face so pinched that not
A star in a stormy spot
  Shows half as much distress.

15.

Did I speak ? did she answer aught ?
 O God ! had I said
" Aimee, 't is I ! " but naught !—
And the mist and the moon distraught
Stared with me on her—dead. . . .

16.

This is the tale they tell
 Of the Hallowe'en ;
This is the thing that befell
Me and the village Belle,
 Beautiful Aimee Dean.

MATER DOLOROSA.

THE nuns sing, "*ora pro nobis*,"
    The lancets glitter above ;
And the beautiful Virgin whose robe is
    Woven of infinite love,
Infinite love and sorrow,
    Prays for them there on high ;—
Who has most need of her prayers,—to-morrow
    Shall tell them,—they or I ?

Up in the hills together
    We loved, where the world seemed true ;
Our world of the whin and heather,
    Our skies of a nearer blue,
A blue from which one borrows
    A faith that helps one die—
O Mother, sweet Mother of Sorrows,
    None needs such more than I !

We lived, we loved unwedded—
  Love's sin and its shame that slays !—
No ill of the year we dreaded,
  No day of its coming days ;
Its coming days, their many
  Trials by morn and night,
And I know no land, not any,
  Where love's lilies grow so white !

Was he false to me, my Mother !
  Or I to him, my God !—
Who gave thee right, O brother !
  To take God's right and rod !
God's rod of avenging morrows,
  And the life here in my side !
O Mother, God's Mother of Sorrows,
  For both I would have died !

By the wall of the Chantry kneeling,
  I pray and the organ rings,
" *Gloria ! gloria !* " pealing,
  " *Sancta Maria* " sings !

They will find us dead to-morrow
　By the wall of their nunnery,
O Mother, sweet Mother of Sorrow !
　His unborn babe and me.

THE OLD INN.

I.

RED-WINDING from the sleepy town,
  One takes the lone, forgotten lane
Straight through the hills. A brush-bird brown
  Bubbles in thorn-flowers sweet with rain ;
  Light shivers sink the gleaming grain ;
The cautious drip of higher leaves
  The lower dips that drip again.—
Above the tangled tops it heaves
Its gables and its haunted eaves.

2.

One creeper, gnarled to bloomlessness,
  O'er-forests all its eastern wall ;
The sighing cedars rake and press
  Dark boughs along the panes they sprawl ;
  While, where the sun beats, breaks a drawl

Of hiving wasps ; one bushy bee,
　Gold-dusty, hurls along the hall
To hum into a crack.—To me
The shadows seem too scared to flee.

3.

Of ragged chimneys martins make
　Huge pipes of music ; twittering here
Build, breed, and roost.—My footfalls wake
　Strange stealing echoes, till I fear
　I 'll meet my pale self coming near ;
My phantom face as in a glass ;
　Or one men murdered, buried—where ?
Dim in gray, stealthy glimmer, pass
With lips that seem to moan " Alas."

LAST DAYS.

AYE! heartbreak of the tattered hills,
    And mourning of the raining sky!
Heartbreak and mourning, since God wills,
    Are mine, and God knows why!

The brutal wind that herds the storm
In hail-big clouds that freeze along,
As this gray heart are doubly warm
    With thrice the joy of song.

I held one dearer than each day
Of life God sets in limpid gold—
What thief hath stole that gem away
    To leave me poor and old!

The heartbreak of the hills be mine,
Of trampled twig and mired leaf,
Of rain that sobs through thorn and pine
    An unavailing grief!

6

The sorrow of the childless skies'
Good-nights, long said, yet never said,
As when I kissed my child's blue eyes
And lips ice-dumb and dead.

THE ROMANZA.

IN a kingdom of mist and moonlight,
  Or ever the world was known,
Past leagues of unsailed water,
There reigned a king with a daughter
  That shone like a starry stone.

The day grew out o' the moonlight ;
  But never a day was there.
The king was wise as hoary,
And his daughter, like the glory
  Of seven kingdoms, fair.

And the night dimmed over the moonlight,—
  And ever the mist was gray,—
With slips of dull stars, bluer
Where the princess met her wooer,
  A page like the month o' May.

In her eyes the mist, and the moonlight
  In hair of a crumpled gold ;
By day they wooed a-hawking,
A-hawking laughed, a-mocking
  The good, white king and old.

On the sea the mist, and the moonlight
  Poured pale to the lilies' tips ;—
At eve, when the hawks were feeding,
In courts to the kennels leading,
  He kissed her mouth and lips.

On towers the mist, and the moonlight
  On a dead face staring up ;—
His kingly couch was ready,
But and her hand was steady
  Giving the poisoned cup.

MY ROMANCE.

IF it so befalls that the midnight hovers
   In mist no moonlight breaks,
The leagues of years my spirit covers,
   And myself myself forsakes.

And I live in a land of stars and flowers,
   White cliffs by a silver sea ;
And the pearly points of her opal towers
   From the mountains beckon me.

And I think that I know that I hear her calling
   From a casement bathed with light—
The music of waters in waters falling
   To palms from a rocky height.   ·

And I feel that I think my love 's awaited
   By the romance of her charms ;
That her feet are early and mine belated
   In a world that chains my arms.

But I break my chains and the rest is easy—
  In the shadow of the rose
Snow-white, that blooms in her garden breezy,
  We meet and no one knows.

To dream sweet dreams and kiss sweet kisses ;
  The world—it may live or die ;
The world that forgets, the soul that misses
  The life that has long gone by.

We speak old vows that have long been spoken,
  And weep a long-gone woe,—
For you must know our hearts were broken
  Hundreds of years ago.

THE EPIC.

"TO arms!" the battle bugles blew.
   The daughter of their Earl was she,
Lord of a thousand swords and true ;
   He but a squire of low degree.

The horns of war blew up to horse :
   He kissed her mouth ; her face was white ;
" God grant they bear thee back no corse ! "—
   " God give I win my spurs to-night ! "

Each watch-tower's blazing beacon scarred
   A blood-blot in the wounded dark :
She heard knights gallop battleward,
   And from the turret leaned to mark.

" My God, deliver me and mine !
   My child ! my God ! " all night she prayed :
She saw the battle beacons shine ;
   She saw the battle beacons fade.

They brought him on a bier of spears.—
    For him—the death-won spurs and name ;
For her—the sting of secret tears,
    And convent walls to hide her shame.

THE BLIND HARPER.

A ND thus it came my feet were led
  To wizard walls that hairy hung
Old as their rock the moss made dead ;
 And, like a ditch of fire flung
Around it, uncouth flowers red
 Thrust spur and fang and tongue.

And here I harped. Did dead men list ?
 Or was it hollow hinges gnarred
Huge, iron scorn in donjon-twist ?
 And when I thought a face sword-scarred
Would curse me, lo ! a woman kissed
 At me hands ringed and starred.

And so I sang ; for she had leaned
 Rare beauty to me, dark and tall ;
I sang of Love, whose Court is queened
 Of Aliénor the virginal,

Nor saw how rolled on me a fiend
   Wolf-eyeballs from the wall.

Oh, how I sang ! until she laughed
   Red lips that made lute harmony ;
I sang of knights who fought and quaffed
   To Love's own paragon, Marie—
Nor saw the suzerain whose shaft
   Was bowed and bent on me.

And I had harped until she wept ;
   But when I sang of Ermengarde
Of Anjou,—where her Court is kept
   By brave, by beauty, and by bard,—
She turned a raven there and swept
   Me, like a fury, 'ward.

A bleeding beak had pierced my sight ;
   A crimson claw each cheek had lined ;
One glimpse : wild walls of threatening night
   Heaped raven battlements behind
A moat of blazing serpents bright—
   And then I wandered blind.

ELPHIN.

THE eve was a burning copper,
   The night was a boundless black
Where wells of the lightning crumbled
   And boiled with blazing rack,
When I came to the coal-black castle
   With the wild rain on my back.

Thrice under its goblin towers,
   Where the causey of rock was laid,
Thrice, there at its spider portal,
   My scornful bugle brayed,
But never a warder questioned,—
   An owl's was the answer made.

When the heaven above was blistered
   One scald of blinding storm,
And the blackness clanged like a cavern
   Of iron where demons swarm,

I rode in the court of the castle
  With the shield upon my arm.

My sword unsheathed and certain
  Of the visor of my casque,
My steel steps challenged the donjon
  My gauntlet should unmask ;
But never a knight or varlet
  To stay or slay or ask.

My heels on the stone ground iron,
  My fists on the bolts clashed steel ;—
In the hall, the roar of the torrent,
  In the turret, the thunder's peal ;—
And I found her there in the turret
  Alone by her spinning-wheel.

She spun the flax of a spindle,
  And I wondered on her face ;
She spun the flax of a spindle,
  And I marvelled on her grace ;
She spun the flax of a spindle,
  And I watched a little space.

But nerves of my manhood weakened ;
  The heart in my breast was wax ;
Myself but the hide of an image
  Out-stuffed with the hards of flax :—
She spun and she smiled a-spinning
  A spindle of blood-red flax.

She spun and she laughed a-spinning
  The blood of my veins in a skein ;
But I knew how the charm was mastered,
  And snapped in the hissing vein ;
So she wove but a fiery scorpion
  That writhed from her hands again. .   .   .

Fleeing in rain and in tempest,
  Saw by the cataract's bed,—
Cancers of ulcerous fire,
  Wounds of a bloody red,—
Its windows glare in the darkness
  Eyes of a dragon's head.

PRE-ORDINATION.

SHE bewitched me in my childhood,
  And the witch's charm is hidden—
Far beyond the wicked wildwood
  I shall find it, I am bidden.

She commands me, she who bound me
  With soft sorcery to follow ;
In a golden snare who wound me
  To her bosom's snowy hollow.   .   .   .

Comes a night-dark stallion sired
  Of the wind ; a mare his mother
Whom Thessalian madness fired,
  And the hurricane his brother.

Then my soul delays no longer :
  Though the night around is scowling,
Keenly mount him blacker, stronger
  Than the tempest that is howling.

At our ears wild shadows whistle ;
  Brazen forks the lightning o'er us
Flames ; and huge the thunder's missile
  Bursts behind us, drags before us.

Over fire-scorched fields of stubble ;
  Iron forests dark with wonder ;
Evil marshes black with trouble ;
  Nightmare torrents thundering under :

In the thorn that past us races,
  Harelipped hags like crows are rocking ;
Stunted oaks have dwarf-like faces
  Gnarled that leer an impish mocking :

Rocks, in which the storm is hooting,
  Thrust a humpbacked murder over ;
Bristling heaths, dead thistles shooting,
  Raven-haunted gibbets cover :

Each and all are passed, like water
  Under-rolled into a cavern,
Till we see the Devil's daughter
  Waiting at the Devil's tavern.

And we stay ; I drain the beaker
  In her hand ; the draught is fire ;
World-remembrances grow weaker,
  And my spirit, one desire.

Course it ! course it ! Darkness passes
  Like an uprolled banner tattered ;
Walled before us mountain masses
  Rise like centuries unscattered.

And the storm flies ragged. Slowly
  Comes a moon of copper-color,
And the evil night grows holy,
  Mists the wild ride growing duller.

In the round moon's angry scanning,
  Demon-swift cross spider arches
Of the web-thick bridges spanning
  Chasms of her kingdom's marches.

We have reached her kingdom, olden
  As the sea that sighs its sadness ;
Rocks and trees and sands are golden,
  And the air a golden gladness.

Shapely ingots are the flowers,
 And the waters, amber brightness ;
Gold-bright song-birds in the bowers
 Sing with eyes of diamond whiteness.

And she meets me with a chalice
 Like the Giamschid ruby burning,
And I drain it without malice,
 To her towers of topaz turning.

Many hundred years forgetting
 All that 's earth : within her power
I possess her : naught regretting
 Since each year is as an hour.

AT THE STILE.

YOUNG Harry leapt over the stile and kissed
    her,
  Over the stile the stars a-winking ;
He thought it was Mary—'t was Mary's sister—
  And love hath a way of thinking.

" Thy pail, sweetheart, I will take and carry."—
  Over the stile the stars hang yellow.—
" Just to the spring, my sweetheart Harry."—
  And love is a heartless fellow.

" Thou saidst me *yea* when the frost did shower
  Over the stile from stars a-shiver."—
" I say thee *nay* now the cherry-trees flower,
  And love is taker and giver."

" O false ! thou art false to me, sweetheart ! "—
  Over the stile the stars a-glister.—

" To thee, the stars, and myself, sweetheart,
  I never was aught save Mary's sister.

" Sweet Mary's sister and thou my Harry,
  Her Harry and mine, but mine the weeping :
In a month or twain you two will marry—
  And I in my grave be sleeping."

Alone among the meadows of millet,
  Over the stile the stars pursuing,
Some tears in her pail as she stoops to fill it—
  And love hath a way of doing.

THE ALCALDE'S DAUGHTER.

THE times they had kissed and parted
    That night were over a score ;
Each time that the cavalier started,
    Each time she would swear him o'er.

"Thou art going to Barcelona !—
    To make Naxera thy bride !
Seduce the Lady Yöna !—
    And thy lips have lied ! have lied !

"I love thee ! I love thee, thou knowest !
    And thou shalt not give away
The love to my life thou owest ;
    And my heart commands thee stay !—

"I say thou hast lied and liest !—
    For where is there war in the state ?—
Thou goest, by Heaven the highest !
    To choose thee a fairer mate.

"Wilt thou go to Barcelona
  When thy queen in Toledo is?
To wait on the haughty Yöna,
  When thou hast these lips to kiss?"

And they stood in the balcony over
  The old Toledo square :
And weeping she took for her lover
  A red rose out of her hair.

And they kissed farewell ; and higher
  The moon made amber the air :
And she drew for the traitor and liar
  A stiletto out of her hair. . . .

When the night-watch lounged through the quiet
  With the stir of halberds and swords,
Not a bravo was there to defy it,
  Not a gallant to brave with words.

One man, at the corner's turning,
  Quite dead. And they stoop or stand—
In his heart a dagger burning,
  And a red rose crushed in his hand.

AT THE CORREGIDOR'S.

TO Don Odora says Donna De Vine :
  "I yield to thy long endeavor !—
At my balcony be on the stroke of nine,
  And, Signor, am thine forever ! "

This beauty but once had the Don descried
  As she quit the confessional ; followed ;
" What a foot for silk ! a face for a bride—
  Hem—! " the rest Odora swallowed.

And with vows as soft as his oaths were sweet
  Her heart he barricaded ;
And pressed this point with a present meet,
  And that point serenaded.

What else could the enemy do but yield
  To a handsome importuning !
A gallant blade with a lute for shield
  All night at her lattice mooning !

" *Que es estrella !* O lily of girls !
   Here 's that for thy fierce duenna :
A purse of pistoles and a rosary o' pearls
   And gold as yellow as henna.

" She will drop from thy balcony's rail, my sweet !
   My seraph ! this silken ladder ;
And then—sweet then !—my soul at thy feet
   No lover of lovers gladder ! "

And the end of it was !—But I will not say
   How he won to the room of the lady :—
Ah ! to love is life and to live is gay,
   For the rest—a maravedi !

Now comes her betrothed from the wars, and he,
   A Count of the Court Castilian,
A Don Diabolus, sword at knee,
   And moustaches—uncivilian.

And his is a jealous love ; and—for
   He marks that this marriage makes sadder—
He watches, and sees a robber to her,
   Or gallant, ascend a ladder.

So he pushes inquiry unto her room,
  With his naked sword demanding—
An Alquazil with the face of Doom,
  Sure of a stout withstanding.

And weapon to weapon they foined and fought ;
  Diabolus' thrusts were vicious ;
Three thrusts to the floor Odora had brought,
  A fourth was more malicious,

Through the offered bosom of Donna De Vine—
  And this is the Count's condition . . .
Was he right, was he wrong? the question is mine,
  To judge—for the Inquisition.

THE PORTRAIT.

IN some quaint Nürnberg *maler-atelier*
　　Uprummaged.　When　and　where　was　never
　　clear,
Nor yet how he obtained it.　When, by whom
'T was painted—who shall say ? itself a gloom
Resisting inquisition.　I opine
It is a Dürer.　Humph ?—that touch, this line
Are not deniable ; distinguished grace
In the pure oval of the noble face ;
The color badly tarnished.　Half in light
Extend it, so ; incline ; the exquisite
Expression leaps abruptly : piercing scorn,
Imperial beauty ; icy, each a thorn
Of light—disdainful eyes and　.　.　.　well ! no use !
Effaced and but beheld, a sad abuse
Of patience.　Often, vaguely visible,
The portrait fills each feature, making swell
The soul with hope : avoiding face and hair

7

Alive with lively warmth ; astonished there
" Occult substantial ! " you exult, when, ho !
You hold a blur ; an undetermined glow
Dislimns a daub.—Restore ?—ah, I have tried
Our best restorers, all ! it has defied. . . .
Storied, mysterious, say, mayhap a ghost
Lives in the canvas ; hers, some artist lost,
A duchess', haply.   Her he worshipped ; dared
Not tell he worshipped ; from his window stared
Of Nuremburg one sunny morn when she
Passed paged to court.   Her cold nobility
Loved, lived for like a purpose ; seized and plied
A feverish brush—her face ! despaired and died.

The narrow Judengasse ; gables frown
Around a skinny usurer's, where brown
And dirty in a corner long it lay,
Heaped in a pile of riff-raff, such as—say,
Retables done in tempora and old
Panels by Wohlgemuth ; stiff paintings cold
Of martyrs and apostles, names forgot ;
Holbeins and Dürers, say, a haloed lot

Of praying saints, madonnas : such, perchance,
Mid wine-stained purples mothed ; a whole romance
Of crucifixes, rosaries ; inlaid
Arms Saracen-elaborate ; a strayed
Niello of Byzantium ; rich work
In bronze, of Florence ; here a delicate dirk,
There holy patens.

        So, my ancestor,
The first De Herancour, esteemed by far
This piece most precious, most desirable ;
Purchased and brought to Paris.   It looked well
In the dark panelling above the old
Hearth of his room.   The head's religious gold,
The soft severity of the nun face,
Made of the room an apostolic place
Revered and feared.—

        Like some lived scene I see
That Gothic room ; its Flemish tapestry :
Embossed above the aged lintel, shield—
Deep Or-enthistled, in an Argent field
Three Sable mallets—arms De Herancour,
Carved with the torso of the crest that bore,

Outstretched, two mallets. Lozenge-paned, em-
    bayed,
Its slender casements ; on a lectern laid,
A vellum volume of black-lettered text ;
Near by a blinking taper—as if vexed
With silken gusts a nervous curtain sends,
Behind which, maybe, daggered Murder bends ;—
Waxed floors of rosy oak, whereon the red
Torchlight of Medicean wrath is shed,
Down knightly corridors ; a carven couch
Sword-slashed ; dark velvets of the chairs that
    crouch,
It seems, with fright ; clear-clashing near, more
    near,
The stir of searching steel.
                    What find they here ?—
'T is St. Bartholomew's—a Huguenot
Dead in his chair ?—dead ! violently shot
With horror, eyes glued on a portrait there,
Coiling his neck one blood line, like a hair
Of finest fire ; the portrait, like a fiend,—
Looking exalted visitation,—leaned

From its black panel ; in its eyes a hate
Demonic ; hair—a glowing auburn, late
A dim, enduring golden.
                    " Just one thread
Of the fierce hair around his throat," they said,
" Twisting a burning ray, he—staring-dead."

ISMAEL.

ISMAEL, the Sultan, in the Ramazan,
 Girdled with guards and many a yataghan,
Pachas and amins, viziers wisdom-gray,
And holy marabouts, betook his way
Through Mekinez.—Written the angel's word,
Of Eden's Kauther, reads, "Slay! praying the
  Lord!
Pray! slaying the victims!" so the Sultan went,
The Cruel Sultan, with this good intent.

In white bournouse and sea-green caftan clad
First to the mosque.   Long each muezzin had
Summoned the faithful unto prayer and let
The "Allah Akbar!" from each minaret,
Call to their thousand lamps of blazing gold.
Prostrated prayed the Sultan.   On the old
Mosaics of the mosque—whose hollow steamed
With aloes-incense—lean ecstatics dreamed

On Allah and his Prophet, and how great
Is God, and how unstable man's estate.
Conviction on him, in this chanting low
Of Koran texts, the Caliph's passion so
Exalted rose,—lamps of religious awe,
Loud smitings of the everlasting law
On unbelievers,—trebly manifest
The Faith's anointed sword he feels confessed.

So from the mosque, whose arabesques above—
The marvellous work of Oriental love—
Seen with new splendors of Heaven's blue and
    gold,
Applauding all, he, as the gates are rolled
Ogival back to let the many forth,
Cries war to all the unbelieving North.

Soon have they passed the tight bazaar ; along
Close, crooked streets, too narrow for the throng ;
The place of owls and tombs ; the merloned wall,
Camel and steed and ass.   Projecting all
Its towering battlements, his palace gray,

Seraglios and courts, against the day
Lifts, vanishes.   And now, soul-set on hate,
From Mekinez they pass the scolloped gate.

Two dozing beggars, baking each a sore,
Sprawl in the sun the city gate before ;
A leprous cripple and a thief, whose eyes—
Burnt out with burning iron,—as supplies
The law for thieves,—two fly-thick wounds blood-
  raw,
Lifted shrill voices as they heard or saw ;
Praised God, and flung into the dust each face
With words of " victory and Allah's grace
Attend our Caliph, Mouley-Ismael !
Even at the cost of ours his days be well ! "

And grimly smiling as he grimly passed,
" While God most merciful, who is, shall last,—
Now by Es Sirat !—will a liar's word
And thief's prevail or prosper ?—Pray the Lord !—
What ! at your lives' cost ?—my devout intent !
Even as 't is bidden let their necks be bent !—

Though words be pious, evil at the soul
Naught is the prayer !—So let their prayer be
    whole.
Nay ! give them gold ; but when the sequins cease
From the slaves' hands, by these my Soudanese
They die ! " he said ; and even as he said
Rolled in the dust each writhing, withered head.

And frowning westward, as the day grew late,
Four bleeding heads stared from the city gate
'Neath this inscription, for the passer-by,
" There is no virtue but in God the High."

A PRE-EXISTENCE.

AN intimation of some previous life,
  Or dark dream, in the present dim-divined,
Of some uncertain sleep—or lived or dreamed
In some dead life—between a dusk and dawn :

From heathen battles to Toledo's gates,
Far off defined, his corselet and camail,
Damascened armet, shattered ; in an eve's
Anger of brass a galloping glitter, one
Rode arrow-wounded.   And the city caught
A cry before him and a wail behind,
Of walls beleaguered ; battles ; conquered kings ;
Triumphant Taric ; broken Spain and slaves.

And I, a Moslem slave, a miser Jew's,
Housed near the Tagus—squalid and alone
Save for his slave, held dear—to beat and starve—
Leaner than my lank shadow when the moon,

A burning beacon, westerns ; and my bones
A visible hunger ; famished with the fear,
Soul-garb of slaves, I bore him—I, who held
Him soul and self, more hated than his God,
Stood silent ; fools had laughed ; I saw my way.

War-time crops weapons ; and the blade I bought
Was subtly pointed. For, I knew his ways :
The nightly nuptials of his jars of gems
And bags of doublas—oh, I knew his ways.
A shadow, woven in the hangings, hid
Till time said *now ;* gaunt from the hangings stole
Behind him ; humped and stooping so, his heart
Clove through the faded tunic, murrey-dyed ;
Grinned exultation while the grim, slow blood
Drenched black and darkened round the oblong
      wound,
And his old face thinned grayer than morn's
      moon.

Rubies from Badakhshân in rose lights dripped
Slim tears of poppy-purple crystal ; dull,
Red, ember-pregnant, carbuncles wherein

Fevered a captive crimson ; bugles wan
Of cat-eyed hyacinths ; moon-emeralds
With starry greenness stabbed ; in limpid stains
Of liquid lilac, Persian amethysts ;
Fire-opals savage and mesmeric with
Voluptuous flame, long, sweet, and sensuous as
Soft eyes of Orient women ; sapphires beamed
With talismanic violet, from tombs,
Deev-guarded, of primordial Solimans ;
Length-agonized with fire, diamonds of
Golconda—This, a sandaled dervise bare
Seven days, beneath a red Arabian sun,
Seven nights, beneath a round Arabian moon,
Under his tongue ; an Emeer's ransom, held
Of some wild tribe. . . . Bleached in the per-
       ishing waste
A Bedouin Arab found sand-strangled bones,
A skeleton, vulture-torn, fierce in whose skull
One blazing eye—the diamond. At Aleppo
Bartered—a bauble for his desert love.—
Jacinth and Indian pearl, gem jolting gem,
Flashed, rutilating in the irised light,

A rain of splintered fire ; and his head,
Long-haired, white-sunk among them.

Yet I took

All—though his eyes burned in them ; though,
    meseemed,
Each several jewel glared a separate curse. . . .

Well ! dead men work us mischief from the grave.
Richer than all Castile and yet not dare
Drink but from cups of Roman murra, spar
Bowl-sprayed with fibrile gold ! spar sensitive
Of poison ! I, no slave, yet all a slave
To fear a dead fool's malice !—Still, how else !
Feasting within the music of my halls,
While perfumed beauty danced in sinuous robes,
Diaphanous, more silken than those famed
Of loomed Amorgos or of classic Kos,
Draining the unflawed murrhine, Xeres-brimmed,
Had I reeled poisoned, dying wolfsbane-slain !

BEHRAM AND EDDETMA.

AGAINST each prince now she had held her
     own,
An easy victor for the seven years
O'er kings and sons of kings ; Eddetma, she
Who, when much sought in marriage, hating men,
Espoused their ways to win beyond their worth
Through martial exercise and hero deeds :
She, who accomplished in all warlike arts,
Let cry through every kingdom of the kings :—
" Eddetma weds with none but him who proves
Himself her master in the push of arms,
Her suitor's foeman she.   And he who fails,
So overcome of woman, woman-scorned,
Disarmed, dishonored, yet shall he depart,
Brow-bearing, forehead-stigmatized with fire,
' Behold, a freedman of Eddetma this.' "
Let cry, and many princes put to shame,
Pretentious courtiers small in thew and thigh,

Proud-palanquined from principalities
Of Irak and of Hind and farther Sind.
Though she was queenly as that Empress of
The proud Amalekites, Tedmureh, and
More beautiful, yet she had held her own.

To Behram of the Territories, one
Son of a Persian monarch swaying kings,
Came bruit of her and her noised victories,
Her maiden beauty and her warrior strength ;
Eastward he journeyed from his father's court,
With men and steeds and store of wealth and arms,
To the rich city where her father reigned,
Its seven citadels by Seven Seas.
And messengered the monarch with a gift
Of savage vessels wroughten out of gold,
Of foreign fabrics stiff with gems and gold.
Vizier-ambassadored the old king gave
His answer to the suitor :—" I, my son,
What grace have I above the grace of God ?
What power is mine but a material ?
What rule have I unto the substanceless ?

Me, than the shadow of the Prophet's shade
Less, God invests with power but of man ;
Man ! and the right beyond man's right is God's ;
His the dominion of the secret soul—
And His her soul ! Now hath my daughter sworn,
By all her vestal soul, that none shall know
Her but her better in the listed field,
Determining spear and sword.—Grant Fate thy
        trust ;
She hangs her hand upon to-morrow's joust,
A prize to win.—My greeting and farewell."
Informed Eddetma and the lists arose.
Armored and keen with a Chorasmian mace,
Davidean hauberk came she.   Her the prince,
Harnessed in scaly gold Arabian, met ;
So clanged the prologue of the battle.   As
Closer it waxed, Prince Behram, who a while
Withheld his valor,—in that she he loved
Opposed him and beset him, woman whom
He had not scathed for the Chosroës' wealth,—
Beheld his madness ; how he were undone
With shining shame unless he strove withal,
Whirled fiery sword and smote ; the bassinet

Rushed from the haughty face that long had scorned
The wide world's vanquished royalty, and so
Rushed on his own defeat. For like unto
A moon gray clouds have caverned all the eve,
The thunder splits and, virgin triumph, there
She sails a silver aspect, vanquished so
Was Behram by his blow. A wavering strength
Swerved in its purpose ; with no final stroke
Stunned stood he and surrendered ; stared and
       stared,
All his strong life absorbed into her face,
All the wild warrior, arrowed by her eyes,
Tamed, and obedient to lip and look.
Then she on him, as condor on a kite,
Plunged pitiless and beautiful and fierce,
One trophy more to added victories ;
Haled off his arms, amazement dazing him ;
Seized steed and garb, confusion filling him ;
And scoffed him forth brow-branded with his shame.

Dazzled, six days he sat, a staring trance ;
But on the seventh, casting stupor off,
Rose, and the straitness of the case that held

Him as with manacles of knitted fire,
Considered, and decided on a way. . . .

Once when Eddetma with a houri band
Of high-born damsels, under eunuch guard,
In the walled palace pleasaunce took her ease,
Under a myrrh-bush by a fountain side,
Where Afrits' nostrils snorted diamond rain
In scooped cornelian, one, a dim, hoar head,—
A patriarch mid gardener underlings,—
Bent spreading gems and priceless ornaments
Of jewelled amulets of hollow gold
Sweet with imprisoned ambergris and musk ;
Symbolic stones in sorcerous carcanets,
Gem-talismans in cabalistic gold.
Whereon the princess marvelled and bade ask,
What did the elder with his riches there?
Who, questioned, mumbled in his bushy beard,
" To buy a wife withal "; whereat they laughed
As oafs when wisdom stumbles. Quoth a maid,
With orient midnight in her starry eyes,
And tropic music on her languid tongue,
" And what if I should wed with thee, O beard

Grayer than my great-grandfather's, what then?"
"One kiss, no more, and, child, thou wert divorced,"
He; and the humor took them till the birds,
That listened in the spice-tree and the plane,
Sang gayly of the gray-beard and his kiss.

Then quoth the princess, "Thou wilt wed with him
Ansada?" mirth in her two eyes' gazelles,
And gravity bird-nestled in her speech;
And took Ansada's hand and laid it in
The old man's staggering hand, and he unbent
Thin, wrinkled brows and on his staff arose,
Weighed with the weight of many heavy years,
And kissed her leaning on his shaking staff,
And heaped her bosom with an Amir's wealth,
And left them laughing at his foolish beard.

Now on the next day, as she took her ease
With her glad troop of girlhood,—maidens who
So many royal tulips seemed,—behold,
Bowed with white years, upon a flowery sward
The ancient with new jewelry and gems,
Wherefrom the sun coaxed wizard fires and lit
Glimmers in glowing green and pendent pearl,

Ultramarine and beaded, vivid rose ;
And so they stood to wonder, and one asked
As yesternoon wherefore the father there
Displayed his Sheikh locks and the genie gems ?
—" Another marriage and another kiss ?—
What ! doth the tomb-ripe court his youth again ?
O aged, libertine in wish not deed !
O prodigal of wives as well as wealth !
Here stands thy damsel "; trilled the Peri-tall
Diarra with the raven in her hair,
Two lemon-flowers blowing in her cheeks,
And took the dotard's jewels with the kiss
In merry mockery.

   Ere the morrow's dawn,
Bethought Eddetma :   " Shall my handmaidens,
Teasing a gray-beard's whim to wrinkled smiles,
For withered kisses still divide his wealth ?
While I stand idle, lose the caravan
Whose least is notable ?—My right and mine—
Betide me what betides."   .   .   .

   And with the morn
Before the man,—for privily she came,—

Stood habited as of her tire-maids
In humble raiment.   Now the ancient saw
And knew her for the princess that she was,
And kindling gladness of the knowledge made
Two sparkling forges of his deep dark eyes
Beneath the ashes of his priestly brows.
Not timidly she came ; but coy approach
Became the maiden of Eddetma's suite ;
And humbly answered he, "All my old heart !"—
Responsive to her quavering request—
"The daughter of the king did give thee leave ?
And thou wouldst well ?—Then wed with me forth-
        right.
Thy hand, thy lips."   So he arose and gave
Her of barbaric jewelry and gems,
And seized her hand and from her lips the kiss,
When from his age, behold, the dotage fell,
And from the man all palsied hoariness ;
Victorious-eyed and amorous with youth,
A god in ardent capabilities
Resistless held her ; and she, swooning, saw
Gloating the branded brow of Prince Behram.

THE KHALIF AND THE ARAB.

A Transcript.

A MONG the tales, wherein it hath been told,
 In golden letters in a book of gold,
Of Hatim Taï's hospitality,
Who, substanceless in death and shadowy,
Made men his guests upon that mountain top
Whereon his tomb grayed from a thistle crop ;—
A tomb of rock where women hewn of stone,
Rude figures, spread dishevelled hair ; whose moan
From dark to daybreak made the silence cry ;
The camel drivers, being tented nigh,
" Ghouls or hyenas," shuddering would say
But only girls of granite find at day :—

And of that city, Sheddad son of Aad
Built mid the Sebaa sands.—A king who had
Dominion of the world and many kings.—
Builded in pride and power out of things

Unstable of the earth.   For he had read
Of Paradise, and to his soul had said,
" Now in this life the like of Paradise
I 'll build me and the Prophet's may despise,
Knowing no need of that he promises."
So for this city taxed the lands and seas,
And Columned Irem, on a blinding height,
Blazed in the desert like a chrysolite ;
The manner of its building, it is told,
Alternate bricks of silver and of gold :
How Sheddad with his women and his slaves,
His thousand viziers, armored troops as waves
Of ocean countless, God with awful flame—
Shot sheer in thunder on him—God, his shame
Confounded and abolished, ere his eyes
Had glimpsed bright follies of that Paradise ;
Lay blotted to a wilderness the land
Accurséd, and the city lost in sand :
Among such tales—who questions of their sooth ?—
One is recorded of an Arab youth :

The Khalif Hisham ben Abdulmelik
Hunting one day, by some unwonted freak

Rode parted from his retinue and gave
Chase to an antelope.   Without or slave,
Amir or vizier to a pasture place
Of sheep he came, where dark, in tattered grace,
Watched one, an Arab youth.   And as it came
The antelope drew off, with mouth of flame
And tongue of fire to the youth he turned
Shouting, " Ho ! fellow ! in what school hast learned !
Seest not the buck escapes me ? worthless one !
O desert dullard ! "

                  Rising in the sun,
" O ignorant," he said, " of that just worth
Of those the worthy of our Muslim earth !
In that thou look'st upon me—what thou art !—
As one fit for contempt, thou lack'st no part
Of my disdain ?—Allah ! I would not own
A dog of thine for friend no other known—
Of speech a tyrant, manners of an ass ! "
And flung him, rags and rage, into the grass.

Provoked, astonished, wrinkled angrily,
Hissed Hisham, " Slave ! thou know'st me not I
    see ! "

Calmly the youth, "Aye, verily I know,
O mannerless ! thy tongue hath told me so,
Thy tongue commanding ere it spake me *peace*—
Soon art thou known, nor late may knowledge
    cease."

"O dog ! I am thy Khalif ! by a hair
Thy life hangs rav'ling."

             " May it dangle there
Till thou art rotted !—Whiles, upon thy head
Misfortunes shower !—Of his dwelling place,
Allah, be thou forgetful !—What ! his grace
Hisham ben Merwan, king of many words—
Few generosities ! " . . .

          A flash of swords
In drifts of dust and lo ! the Khalif's troops
Surrounding ride. As when a merlin stoops
Some stranger quarry, prey that swims the wind,
Heron or eagle ; kenning not its kind
There whence 't is cast until it, towering, feels
An eagle's tearing talons, falling reels
In broken circles downward—so the youth,

An Arab fearless as the face of Truth
Of all that made him instant of his death,
Waited with eyes indifferent, equal breath.

The palace reached, "Bring in the prisoner
Before the Khalif," and he came as were
He in no wise concerned : unquestioning went
Chin bowed on breast, and on his feet a bent
Dark gaze of scornful freedom unafraid,
Till at the Khalif's throne his steps were staid ;
And unsaluting, standing head held down,
An armed attendant blazed him with a frown,
" Dog of the Bedouins ! thy eyes rot out !
Insulter ! must the whole big world needs shout
'Commander of the Faithful,' so thou see ? "

To him the Arab sneering, "Verily,
Packsaddle of an ass."

                        The Khalif's rage
Exceeded now, and, " By my realm and rage !
Arab, thy hour is come, thy very last ;
Thy hope is vanished and thy life is past."

The shepherd answered, "Aye ?—by Allah, then,
O Hisham, if my time be stretched again,
Unscissored of what Destiny ordain,
Little or great, thy words give little pain."

Then the chief Chamberlain, " O vilest one
Of all the Arabs ! wilt thou not be done
Bandying thy baseness with the Ruler of
The Faithful ?" spat upon his face.   A scoff
Fiery made answer :

   " There be some have heard
The nonsense of our God, the text absurd,
'One day each soul whatever shall be prompt
To bow before me and to give accompt.'"

Then wroth indeed was Hisham ; hotly said,
" He braves us !—headsman, ho ! his peevish head !
See ; canst thou medicine its speech anew,
Doctor its multiplying words to few ;
Divorce them well."   So, where the Arab stood,
Bound him ; made kneel upon the cloth of blood :
With curving sword the headsman leaned at pause,

And, even as 't is custom made of laws,
To the descendant of the Prophet quoth,
"O Khalif, shall I strike?"

          "By Iblis' oath!
Strike!" answered Hisham; but again the slave
Questioned; and yet again the Khalif gave
His nodded "yea"; and for the third time then
He asked—and knowing neither men nor Jinn
Might save him if the Khalif spake assent,
Signalled the sword, the youth with body bent
Laughed—till the wang-teeth of each jaw appeared,
Laughed—as with scorn the King of kings he 'd
    beard,
Insulting death.   So, with redoubled spleen
Roared Hisham rising, "It is truly seen
That thou art mad who mockest Azrael!"

The Arab answered: "Listen!—Once befell,
Commander of the Faithful, that a hawk,
A hungry hawk, pounced on a sparrow-cock;
And winging nestward with his meal in claw,
To him the sparrow, for the creature saw

The hawk's conceit, addressed this slyly, 'Oh,
Most great, most royal, there is not, I know,
That in me which will stay thy stomach's stress,
I am too paltry for thy mightiness ' ;
With which the hawk was pleased, and flattered so
In his self-praise, he let the sparrow go."

Then smiled the Khalif Hisham ; and a sign
Staying the scimitar, that hung malign
A threatening crescent, said, "God bless, preserve
The Prophet whom all true believers serve !—
Now by my kinship to the Prophet, and
Had he at first but spake us thus this hand
Had ne'er been reckless, and instead of hate
He had had all—except the Khalifate."
Bade stuff his mouth with jewels and entreat
Him courteously, then from the palace beat.

THE END.